MAGICAL CHRISTMAS STORIES

Edited by Anne Finnis

André Deutsch · Children's Books

Scholastic Children's Books
7–9 Pratt Street, London NW1 0AE, UK
a division of Scholastic Ltd
London ~ New York ~ Toronto ~ Sydney ~ Auckland

First published by Scholastic Ltd, 1995

This anthology copyright © Scholastic Ltd, 1995

ISBN 0 590 54202 8

Typeset by TW Typesetting, Midsomer Norton, Avon
Printed by Clays Ltd, St Ives plc

Acknowledgements

All of the stories are original and appear for the first time in this volume.

The following are the copyright owners of the stories:

The Pirates' Christmas Party copyright © 1995 Adèle Geras

The Box of Magic copyright © 1995 Malorie Blackman

The Smallest Christmas Tree copyright © 1995 Mary Dickinson

The Wishing Star copyright © 1995 Ruth Silvestre

The Last Mince Pie copyright © 1995 Tessa Krailing

Jamie's Special Delivery copyright © 1995 Elizabeth Lindsay

The Christmas Shawl copyright © 1995 Sue Stops

Florence copyright © 1995 Ann Ruffell

The Caretaker's Christmas copyright © 1995 Malcolm Yorke

When Every Day Was Christmas copyright © 1995 Jean Ure

The Green Mouse copyright © 1995 Gillian Cross

Contents

The Pirates' Christmas Party

Adèle Geras

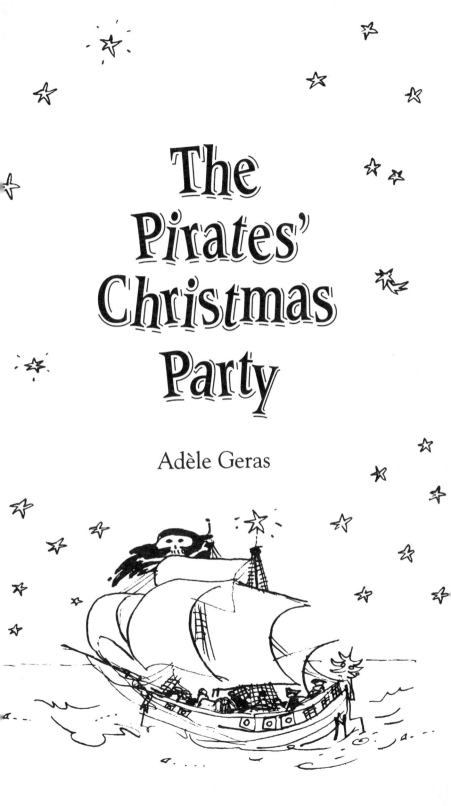

"After you've both finished your pudding," said Beth, "you can listen to what I wrote at school today. It was so good that Mrs Barnes made me read it out in front of the whole class."

"What have we done to deserve it?" said Andy, Beth's brother, and their mother said: "Be quiet, Andy. We listen to you often enough, going on and on about this and that." She smiled at Beth. "We'd love to hear it."

"What's it about?" said Andy, sighing. "Go on, get it over with."

"It's called 'My Best Christmas Present Ever'. Are you ready? I'll stand up so that you can hear me properly."

"We're all together round the table," said Mum. "We're not in the Albert Hall. I think you can stay sitting down."

"I'll go and get it out of my school bag then," said Beth. "Don't anybody move."

She was back almost at once, holding a big sheet of paper. Andy groaned.

"It's not long, is it?" he said. "Some of us have got stuff to do."

"It's as long as it has to be," said Beth, "to say what I want it to say."

"Get on with it then," said Andy.

"Right," said Beth. "I will." She coughed and sat up very straight in her chair:

" 'My Best Christmas Present Ever' by Beth Johnston. Class 4.

" 'My dad works on an oil-rig, and last year he had to stay on the rig over Christmas. He sent me a present from Scotland. It is a ship in a bottle. The ship is called a galleon. My dad says that ships are always called "she", like girls. She has three masts and lovely white sails, and a figurehead of a red fish with blue eyes. She is very beautiful. My brother Andrew is ten years old, and he likes pirates. He said she was a pirate ship. Dad said I could call her anything I wanted, so I decided on "The Crimson Cod". I put the bottle with the ship in it on the table next to my bed, and when I go to sleep, I wish I could get very tiny and wake up on board the galleon, as a cabin-girl.'

"There." Beth beamed at her mother and brother. "What did you think of that?"

"Not bad," said Andy, "and quite short, really."

"It was lovely!" said Mum. "Keep it to show Dad when he gets back tomorrow. Now, who's going to help me with the dishes?"

The last thing Beth did before she got into bed was open a door on her advent calendar. December 14th. Tomorrow was the last day of school. There would be turkey and roast potatoes in the canteen, and everyone singing carols in the afternoon. Then came the ten days before Christmas: the best ten days of the year. Beth loved choosing gifts and making decorations and finding exactly the right tree, and writing Christmas cards and wrapping all the presents in special paper covered with pictures of Santa and his reindeer. She longed to make a snowman, and wished they lived in a colder part of the country.

Beth spent a lot of time wishing and when she wasn't wishing, she was imagining. Sometimes she pretended she was a princess, and sometimes that she was one of King Arthur's knights. Sometimes she imagined that she lived in the dolls' house under the window, and was friends with all her dolls, but the very best games of all were the ones she played with Andy. He didn't play with her as often as she would have liked, but the Pirate Game was Beth's favourite. Andy said that "Andrew" wasn't a very piratical name, so he became Captain Cutlass Caleb and she was his trusty cabin-girl, Buccaneer Beth.

She lay in bed and turned on her side so that she could look at the Crimson Cod, safe in her bottle. Someone had painted green and blue waves on the glass, so that it really looked as though the little galleon were flying through the water. Perhaps, thought Beth, they were on their way to search for buried treasure. She closed her eyes. Suddenly, it seemed as though her whole bed was rocking gently to and fro...

Beth sat up. She blinked and rubbed her eyes. Where was her bedroom? What had happened to her bed? And why wasn't she wearing her pyjamas with spacemen on them? She seemed to be in a hammock, in a long, low room, dimly lit by one lantern. There were other hammocks, slung from beams in the ceiling, and in them Beth could see...

"Pirates!" she cried aloud, and rolled out of her hammock and on to the floor. "You're all pirates!

I'm on a pirate ship. Wake up, please! Help!" She could hear snores all around her.

She peered into the nearest hammock and saw a pink-faced man with a long, ginger beard, sleeping with his mouth open. She prodded him.

"Avast, me hearties…" he mumbled, and opened his eyes. "Oh, 'tis you, Buccaneer Beth. Pass me the rum, there's a good cabin-girl."

"Who are you?" asked Beth. The ginger beard shook and wobbled while the pirate laughed.

"I'm Ginger George," he said, "as well you know, Beth m'dear." The other pirates began to wake up. Beth decided to watch and listen and pretend that she knew exactly what was going on. I'm dreaming, she said to herself. I was looking at the Crimson Cod before I fell asleep and now I'm dreaming that I'm aboard a pirate ship. I shall wake up soon, so I'm not going to worry.

Breakfast on board a pirate ship turned out to be hard biscuits dipped in cold beer.

"Don't you have cornflakes?" Beth asked

Ginger George. "Or toast and marmalade?"

"Them's for landlubbers," said Fearsome Four-Eye Fergal, a skinny pirate who wore glasses and didn't seem fearsome at all.

After breakfast, Beth followed the others up on deck.

" 'Tis time," said Fergal, "to swab the decks and mizzen the main mast and swizzle the sails." Beth had never heard of swizzling the sails, so she pointed to a small, round man in a red coat. He had an eye-patch and a long twirly moustache. Beth said:

"Is that the Captain?"

"You know it is," Fergal answered. "That's Black-Hearted Basil, the Scourge of the Seven Seas and Captain of the Crimson Cod."

"Are we sailing on the Crimson Cod?" Beth wanted to know.

"You're asking more daft questions than there's weevils in the flour, lass. Surely you know what your own ship is called?"

Beth said nothing. A terrible thought occurred to her. What if she weren't dreaming? What if there really *was* such a thing as wishes coming true? What if she truly *was* on board a pirate ship? Would she ever get back to her real life? For a moment she felt like crying. I'm never going to make a wish again, she said to herself. And what about Christmas? She said to Fergal: "Are we going to do anything exciting for Christmas?"

"Never do," said Fergal. "Not as long as I've been at sea."

"No presents?"

"No."

"No turkey or mince pies?"

"No."

"Don't you hang out your stockings on Christmas Eve?" Fergal shook his head.

"What about singing carols?"

"We sing sea-shanties," said Fergal. "Never heard of no carols."

"I wish," said Beth, "to see the Captain."

"The Captain's a busy man," said Fergal. "I doubt he'll have the time to bandy words with the likes o' you."

Beth, however, was quite determined to speak to Black-Hearted Basil and so Fergal led her to his cabin door. She knocked on it three times.

"Enter!" said a pleasant, rather soft voice.

Beth opened the door, and tried not to stare. Black-Hearted Basil was sitting on a sofa, knitting. Beside him was a gigantic white, fluffy cat who looked just like a round cushion that had had two green eyes sewn on to it. All around the cabin were straw baskets overflowing with balls of wool in every colour you could possibly imagine, and there was an embroidery frame in one corner, where Basil had just started work on a tapestry. The picture painted on the canvas was of a country cottage and a garden full of flowers. Beth looked at it in amazement.

"You're admiring my tapestry, I see," said Basil. "It's a new hobby of mine. I've only ever done knitting and crochet before, so I thought I'd branch out."

"I never knew," said Beth, "that pirates did things like knitting."

"Well, the days at sea are endlessly long, my duck, and there's only so much swabbing and mizzening and shinning up the rigging that a chap can do all at once."

"But what about boarding other ships and stealing their cargo? Burying treasure and making maps of where it's to be found? What about making people walk the plank?" Beth sounded quite plaintive.

"Oh, we do all those things occasionally of course. When the need arises, you might say. But it does still leave me an awful lot of time to pursue my hobbies. Do you like what I'm making now?" He held up his knitting so that Beth could see it better. "It's a fiendishly difficult Fair Isle pattern, but this waistcoat will be a thing of beauty, mark my words."

Beth coughed. If she didn't say something soon, the Captain would keep her there discussing knitting patterns for ages. She said:

"Please, sir, I'd like to organize a Christmas party."

"Christmas?" The Captain counted off a few stitches and muttered to himself for a moment. "Is it Christmas already?"

"Yes, sir, and I think we should have a party. We could decorate the ship, and the Cook could make a cake, and we could sing carols. I don't suppose we could get hold of a Christmas tree, but I'm sure everyone would love a party."

The Captain sucked the end of a knitting needle and said: "Decorations ... decorations ... that rings a bell ... I'm sure that somewhere in here..." He smiled at Beth. "Please forgive me. I've been at sea so long that I've forgotten what some of these old chests have actually got in them, only I have a distinct memory of my old mum saying something about Christmas, last time she packed my sea-chests. Let's have a little look."

Black-Hearted Basil laid his knitting down on the sofa.

"Morgan," he said to the cat, "don't you dare chew my wool." Morgan yawned as though wool-chewing would be altogether too much effort, and closed his eyes for a nap. Black-Hearted Basil began to rummage, first in one chest, then in another.

"Here we are!" he cried at last. "I knew it! Here's enough decorations for an entire fleet of ships!"

Beth couldn't believe her eyes. There were rolls of tinsel, coloured glass balls, paper lanterns, yards and yards of red ribbon, little bottles full of glitter, a bag full of assorted gold and silver stars, plastic holly and mistletoe, and right at the bottom of the chest, a little Christmas tree, carefully wrapped up in a polythene bag.

"That's my mum all over," said Basil. "She thinks of everything. Real Christmas trees shed their needles all over the carpet, but this little imitation one … well, it's quite lovely, don't you agree?"

"It's perfect," said Beth. "Now we can have a really wonderful Christmas party. I shall go and talk to the Cook at once."

"And I shall summon the crew on to the deck and address them all. I don't do that very often and I shall enjoy it. Come and listen, before you go down and talk to Cook."

Beth and the Captain went up on deck. The First Mate, Desperate Bertie, rang the bell that called the pirates from every corner of the Crimson Cod. When they had all gathered into a raggedy crowd, Black-Hearted Basil raised his hand for silence.

"Our esteemed cabin-girl, Buccaneer Beth, has had a splendid idea. We are going to have a Christmas Party!"

The crew cheered loudly, and several of the pirates threw their caps in the air and whistled.

"Now," the Captain continued, "has anyone got anything at all Christmassy tucked away in their sea-going bundles? I want you all to have a good look and tell young Beth what you come up with… We will all assemble here again in one hour."

The pirates hurried away to look through their belongings. After an hour, they came up on deck once more, and Beth made a list of everything they had found. The list read:

1 box of assorted crackers - Peg-leg Percy.
2 boxes of mixed streamers - Browntooth Billy.
1 set of angel chimes (with candles) - One-arm Eric.
3 sets of paper napkins (holly and bells pattern) - Jabez the Knife.
1 fairy doll (for top of tree) - Silent Angus.
1 Santa Claus costume - Ginger George.
1 mouth organ - Fearsome Fergal.

"That's a very good list," said Beth. "Thank you all very much indeed."

"I'll tell you what I've found," said Desperate Bertie, "and that's a bundle of knitted stockings. The Captain tried to interest me in knitting, aargh, a good few years ago now, but I only ever got the hang of stockings. P'raps we can hang 'em on our hammocks, come Christmas Eve, and Ginger George can dress up in that there costume of his, and fill 'em all with ship's biscuits!"

"What a good idea, Bertie!" said Beth. "Please go and find them. Each man at the party can have one and that will be their going-home present. You can't have a proper party without a present to take home. We'll get Ginger George to give them out."

The next few hours were spent in frantic preparations. Cross-Eyed Colin, the Cook of the Crimson Cod, (who never left his kitchen, even in a Force Ten gale) had been persuaded to open his secret larder, and in it there were enough good things to make:

1 enormous fruit cake.

24 mince pies.

2 gallons of brandy sauce.

The younger members of the crew climbed the rigging and tied coloured tinsel to the tops of the sails. They fixed the biggest gold star of all to the very top of the tallest mast, where it caught the sun and twinkled brightly enough to dazzle the passing sea birds. Down on the deck, a big spare sail was unrolled and spread out like a table cloth, and Jabez the Knife (who had once done a three-week course in Flower Arrangement) had decorated the table with sprigs of imitation holly and paper napkins in the shape of roses. There was a cracker beside every plate, and the angel chimes made a pretty centre-piece. The Captain's Christmas tree, with Silent Angus's fairy doll right at the top of it, stood on an upturned bucket, which had been cunningly covered in red crêpe paper to make it look festive. Cross-Eyed Colin ventured up on deck for the first time in years to set out the food, and Beth poured rum into every glass.

When all the pirates had sat down, Beth said:

"The first thing we must do is pull our crackers and put on our paper hats."

This took some time, while the pirates giggled and shrieked and swapped hats with one another, because there were some people who didn't think blue suited them, and others who said they'd rather not wear orange, thank you very much.

Then came the eating and drinking. Everyone agreed it was the best feast ever to be spread on the deck of the Crimson Cod. There wasn't a single pirate who didn't have to loosen his waistband before long, and Ginger George, magnificent in his Santa Claus outfit, began muttering about going on a diet. Beth stood up. She said:

"Thank you all very much for helping to make this such a lovely party. Before Ginger George gives you all your knitted stockings as a present,

I'd like you to join in with this Christmas sea-shanty I've made up. It's very easy to learn."

"Yes!" shouted the pirates. "Sing us a Christmas shanty, lass!"

Beth coughed a little and began to sing:

"Paper hats and a spring of holly,
a cracker to pull with a yo-ho-ho.
Tinsel on the sails looks oh, so jolly.
It's Christmas time, so yo-heave-ho.

Fill our Christmas stockings with nice surprises,
yo-ho-ho and a bell to ring.
Nuts and oranges and fat mince pie-ses.
Sing a Christmas shanty, boys!
Sing, sing, sing!"

Fergal took up the tune on his mouth-organ, and soon all the pirates were singing loudly enough to shiver the timbers of the Crimson Cod.

After the singing, Ginger George went and found his sack, and the pirates lined up for their gift of one knitted stocking each. Beth said to Bertie:

"They're really beautiful, Bertie. You never told me they were stripy."

"Oh, aye," said Bertie. "Not much point to a stocking, unless it's striped. That's what my Auntie Maud always used to say."

"May I have one as well?" Beth asked.

"Of course," said Ginger George, plunging his hand into the sack. "What do you say to stripes of purple and green?"

"Thank you," said Beth. "I'll keep it as a souvenir of the party."

In the end, even the fiercest pirate has to go to bed. Beth climbed into her hammock, clutching her knitted stocking. The Crimson Cod rocked gently on the waves, and Beth fell asleep almost at once.

Suddenly someone was shouting in her ear.

"Come on, lazy Beth!" said her mum's voice. "School today, you know. You can't lie in until tomorrow."

Beth opened her eyes and knew at once that she was back in her own bedroom.

"I dreamed I was on a pirate ship last night…" she started to say, but Mum was already on her way downstairs.

"Tell me about it later," she called over her shoulder.

Beth washed and dressed. Then she looked down at the Crimson Cod, lying quietly in her glass bottle. Something was glittering at the top of the main mast, and Beth picked up the bottle to have a closer look. There, for anyone to see, was a tiny gold star.

"It *was* true," Beth whispered to herself. "I *did* sail on a pirate ship." She shook her head and blinked her eyes and looked again. The gold star was still there. Maybe she'd tell Andy about it all later. He'd believe her. She didn't think anyone else would. Beth thought: we won't say a word about it to other people ... it'll be our secret, Andy's and mine. She put the bottle with the Crimson Cod in it back on the table and went downstairs smiling to herself.

Later that morning, Beth's mother was tidying up her daughter's room. She found what looked like a doll's stocking on the floor beside the bed. It had been hand-knitted in thin stripes of purple and green. Beth's mum put it away in the dolls' house, wondering, not for the first time, where Beth found some of the things that ended up among her toys.

The Box
of
Magic

Malorie Blackman

It was Christmas Eve, but Peter was in no hurry. His head bent, Peter dragged his feet as he made his way slowly home. There was no point in rushing. Mum and Dad would only be arguing about something or another. Peter and his sister Chloe had hoped that the quarrelling would stop over Christmas. It hadn't. If anything, it'd got worse.

Peter had spent all afternoon searching and searching for the perfect present for his mum and dad. Something that would stop them quarrelling for just five minutes. Something that would make Christmas the way it used to be, with smiles and songs and happiness in every corner of the house. But all the searching had been for nothing. Peter didn't have that much money to begin with and all the things he could afford, he didn't want. All the gifts he could afford looked so cheap and tacky that Peter knew they would fall apart about ten seconds after they were handled. What was he going to do? He had to buy something and time was running out.

Then he caught sight of it out of the corner of his eye.

The medium-sized sign above the door said "THE CHRISTMAS SHOP" in spidery writing. The small shop window was framed with silver and gold tinsel and a scattering of glitter like mini stars. At the bottom of the window, fake snow had been sprayed. It looked so much like the real thing that had it been outside the window instead of inside, Peter would've been sure it was real snow. A single Christmas tree laden down with fairy lights and baubles and yet more tinsel stood proudly in the exact centre of the window.

Peter stood in front of the shop and stared. He'd never seen anything so … wonderful! It was as if Christmas had started in this shop and then spread out to cover the whole wide world.

"The Christmas Shop…" Peter muttered to himself.

He wondered why he'd never seen it before. True, it was behind the shopping precinct and he usually walked through the precinct not around it, but even so. Peter looked up and down the street. The few other shops in the same row as the Christmas Shop were all boarded up.

Unexpectedly, the shop door opened. A tall portly man with a white beard and a merry twinkle in his eyes stood in the doorway.

"Hello! Come in! Come in!" The shopkeeper beckoned.

"I … er … don't have much money." Peter shook his head.

"No matter. Come in." The shopkeeper turned and held the door open. It was as if there was no doubt in his mind that Peter would enter. Uncertainly, Peter dithered on the pavement. He hadn't intended to go in. He was only window shopping. But the shop looked so warm and inviting and the shopkeeper seemed so friendly. Peter walked into the shop.

And he gasped in amazement!

It was even better inside than it had appeared from outside. It smelt of freshly baked bread and warm cakes and toast and cinnamon and nutmeg and it was so warm it was as if the sun itself had come for a visit.

"Isn't my shop the best!" smiled the shop-keeper. "Look around. Feel free. You can pick up anything, touch anything."

Peter stared at the shopkeeper. He certainly wasn't like any other shopkeeper Peter had ever met. Usually shopkeepers didn't like school kids in their shops and they certainly didn't like them touching things. Peter wandered around the shop, his dark brown eyes wide with delight. Toys and games and Christmas sweets and Christmas treats filled every corner.

Peter's hand curled around the money in his pocket. He could buy all his Christmas presents in here. Peter bent his head to examine a gold and berry-red scarf. That would be perfect for his mum. And maybe the night-blue and yellow scarf for his dad. And he could get that little glass unicorn over there for Chloe. That was just the kind of thing she liked. The strange thing was, none of the items had prices on them.

"H-How much are these woolly scarves?" Peter asked, crossing his fingers in his pockets. "And how much is that unicorn over there?"

"That depends on who they're for and why you think they'd like them," answered the shop-keeper.

"The scarves are for my mum and dad and the unicorn is for my sister. Chloe likes things made of glass. She keeps them in her bedroom on the window sill. And I thought that Mum and Dad could have the scarves to keep them warm."

"And how much money do you have?" asked the shopkeeper.

Peter took out all the money in his pocket. The shopkeeper checked through it carefully.

"You're lucky," said the shopkeeper. "You've got enough for all the things you want."

"I have? Really?" Peter couldn't believe it.

The shopkeeper smiled and nodded. Peter grinned at him, but slowly his smile faded. He'd buy the scarves for his dad and mum and then what? What good would any present do? Peter could see it now. Mum and Dad opening their presents on Christmas Day.

"Thanks Peter. That's great," says Dad.

"Peter, that's wonderful," says Mum.

And then they'd fling their presents to the back of the chair and start shouting at each other again.

"What's the matter, Peter?" asked the shop-keeper gently.

Peter jumped. He'd been lost in a world of his own.

"It's just that... Hang on a second. How did you know my name?" Peter stared.

"It's a little game of mine," the shopkeeper beamed. "I like to guess people's names and nine times out of ten, I get it right."

Peter was impressed.

"So you were saying?" the shopkeeper prompted.

"I ... I don't suppose you've got anything in your shop to stop my mum and dad from fighting?" The moment the words were out of his mouth, Peter regretted it. What was he doing? He hadn't told anyone about his mum and dad, not even his best friend Andy. No one knew how things were at home except his sister Chloe and she didn't talk about it either.

"Oh, I see. Do your mum and dad argue a lot?" asked the shopkeeper.

"All the time," Peter sighed.

The shopkeeper pursed his lips. "Hhmm! I think I have just the present you need – for your whole family."

The shopkeeper went around his brightly-coloured counter and disappeared down behind it. Moments later he straightened up, a huge smile on his face and a silver box in his hands.

"These are what you need," he said.

"What are they?" Peter asked doubtfully.

"Christmas crackers," announced the shop-keeper proudly. At the disappointed look on Peter's face, he added, "Ah, but they're not just any crackers. They're magic. Guaranteed to work or your money back."

"How are they magic?" Peter asked suspiciously.

"The magic only works if they're pulled on Christmas Day, when you're all around the table eating dinner," explained the shopkeeper.

"But how do they work?"

"It's hard to explain. You have to see the magic for yourself."

"How much are they?" asked Peter, still doubtful.

Maybe he could buy them and still get the other presents as well.

"I'm afraid they're very expensive because they're magic," said the shopkeeper. "They'll cost you all the money you've got and even then I'm letting you have them cheap."

Peter thought for a moment. Magic crackers. Crackers that would actually stop Mum and Dad from arguing. They were worth the money if they could do that. He took a deep breath.

"All right, I'll take them," he said quickly, before he could change his mind.

Peter handed over his money and the shopkeeper handed over the box of eight crackers. Moments later, Peter was out of the shop and running all the way home. Magic crackers! He couldn't wait for Christmas Day.

"I've been in that kitchen since seven o'clock

this morning. I think the least you could do is sit at the table with the rest of your family." Mum's voice dripped with ice.

"I want to watch the end of this film," Dad argued.

"Typical! You're so selfish," Mum snapped.

Peter and Chloe looked at each other and sighed. Mum and Dad were at it again. Christmas Day – and they were still arguing.

"Dad, you and Mum and Chloe can open my present now," Peter said desperately. "The man in the Christmas Shop said they should only be opened when we're all sitting round the table eating dinner."

"Oh, all right then," Dad grumbled.

"Oh, I see. You'll come to the table if Peter asks you to, but not if I ask you," sniffed Mum.

"Peter doesn't nag me every two seconds," Dad said as he sat down at the table.

Chloe shook her head and turned to look out of the window. Peter ran to get the present he'd bought. It was the only one left unopened under the tree. He stood between his mum and dad, putting the present down on the tablecloth. Mum and Dad looked at each other.

"Go on then," Dad prompted.

"You do it," said Mum.

"I'll do it," said Chloe.

She tore off the bright red and yellow wrapping paper.

"It's a box of crackers," she said, surprised.

"Not just any crackers," Peter said eagerly. "They're *magic* crackers!"

"Who told you that?" Mum smiled.

"The man in the Christmas Shop," Peter replied.

"Well, let's all sit down. Then we can pull them and get on with our dinner," said Dad, adding under his breath, "And maybe then I can get back to my film."

But the moment they all sat down, something peculiar began to happen. A strange feeling settled over the dinner table. A hopeful, expectant feeling – as if, in spite of themselves, everyone was waiting for something terrific, amazing *and* spectacular to happen all at once. The noise from the telly was just a distant hum at the other end of the room. Light like warm spring sunshine came from everyone smiling at everyone else as they watched Dad place two crackers beside each plate. Chloe held out her cracker to Dad. Peter held his Christmas cracker out to Mum.

"One! Two! Three!" they all shouted.

Bang! Pop! The sound of exploding crackers filled the room. Chloe and Peter got the biggest parts of the crackers. They both peered down into them.

"They're … they're *empty*!" Chloe exclaimed.

"No! They can't be," frowned Mum.

"See for yourself," said Chloe, handing over her cracker.

Peter couldn't believe it. Empty… When he

remembered the smiling, friendly face of the jolly man with the white beard in the Christmas Shop, he just *couldn't* believe it. That man wouldn't take his money and sell him a box of *nothing* – Peter was sure he wouldn't. And yet … and yet, his cracker was empty. Just an empty roll covered with some glossy paper and nothing else. No hats. No jokes. No gifts. Nothing.

"Maybe there were just two duff ones in the box," Mum suggested.

Mum and Dad pulled their crackers next. The same thing happened. They were empty. Chloe and Peter pulled crackers five and six at the same time as Mum and Dad pulled crackers seven and eight.

They were all empty.

Peter examined each one, hoping against hope that they'd got it wrong or it was a trick – but it wasn't. Peter looked at Chloe, then Mum and Dad – and burst into tears. He couldn't help it.

"The shopkeeper told me they were magic crackers," Peter sobbed to Mum and Dad. "I only bought them because he said they would make you stop arguing with each other. He promised me they were magic. He *promised* me…"

Dad stared. Mum's mouth fell open.

"You … you bought them – because of *us*?" Dad asked, aghast.

Peter sniffed and nodded.

"Never mind, Peter." Chloe put her arm around her younger brother's shoulder. "Besides, nothing would stop Mum and Dad from fighting. Not even a real box of magic crackers." And with that, Chloe burst into tears too.

"Chloe! Peter!" Mum and Dad ran around the table to hug Peter and Chloe to them. "We had no idea we were quarrelling that much."

"And we had no idea we were upsetting both of you so much," said Dad.

But Peter and Chloe couldn't stop crying.

"I'll tell you what," said Mum. "Let's make our

own Christmas crackers. All this food will stay warm in the oven until we've finished."

"Terrific idea." Dad went over to the telly and switched it off. "We'll make the hats first," Dad continued. "Out of newspaper."

Dad and Mum showed Peter and Chloe how to make sailor hats out of newspaper. That took about five minutes. Then they all sat down for dinner. Over dinner, everyone had to tell the worst jokes they knew, like, "How do you make an apple puff? Chase it round the garden!" and "Why did the elephant cross the road? Because it was the chicken's day off!" Dad's joke was "Why did silly Billy stand on a ladder when he was learning to sing? So he could reach the high notes!" And Mum's joke was ancient but she was still proud of it! "How do you make a Swiss Roll? Push him down a hill!" Chloe told a joke that Peter didn't get until Mum explained it. "How do you tell how old a telephone is? Count its rings!" (Mum explained that you could tell the age of a tree by counting the rings through its trunk.) Everyone got Peter's joke. "Why are vampires crazy? Because they're often bats!" And when anyone ran out of jokes, they made them up, which was even funnier!

After dinner when everyone was eating Christmas pudding, Mum grabbed Dad and whispered in his ear. Suddenly they both dashed off upstairs with the empty crackers. Ten minutes later they reappeared with the various ends of each cracker now glued together.

"Cracker time!" said Mum. And she held out a cracker to Chloe.

They both pulled.

"POP!" shouted Mum.

Chloe looked inside the cracker and there was one of Mum's old bangles – the gold and blue one which had always been Chloe's favourite.

"Your turn," said Dad, holding out a cracker to Peter. They both shouted, "BANG!"

Peter looked inside the cracker. There was a pig

made of lego bricks. At least, that's what Peter thought it was.

"It's not a pig. It's a rocket!" said Dad, indignantly.

Mum started to giggle. "I told you it looked more like a pig, dear," she said.

They "popped" the rest of the crackers. They all had very silly, very tacky, very wonderful presents in them.

"Who needs rotten, mouldy old crackers?" asked Dad. "We can do it all ourselves."

"And they're much better too," Mum agreed. "It's just a shame that Peter got conned out of his money. Where did you say the shop was?"

"Behind the precinct. All the other shops on the same street were boarded up," Peter replied.

"There aren't any shops behind the precinct. The last one closed down over a year ago," Dad frowned.

"There's one still open. It's called the Christmas Shop," said Peter.

Mum and Dad looked at each other. They both shrugged.

"Never mind. I'd say they were the best crackers we've ever had," smiled Mum. "My jaw still aches from laughing at all those terrible jokes."

"Those crackers were … a box of magic," said Dad, giving Mum a cuddle.

Later that night, as Peter lay in bed, he still couldn't quite believe what had happened. Mum and Dad hadn't argued once since the crackers had been pulled. In fact it was the most wonderful day they'd all had in a long, long time. The only cloud was the shopkeeper who'd sold Peter the crackers in the first place. Peter still didn't want to believe that the shopkeeper was a crook who had deliberately diddled him out of his money.

A strange tinkling-clinking came from across the room, followed by a plopping sound. Peter sat up and frowned. What was that? He switched on his bedside light. There it was again – the same strange noise. And it seemed to be coming from his chair over by the window. Over the back of the chair were the jumper and the pair of trousers Peter had worn on Christmas Eve. That strange noise couldn't be coming from them – could it? Swallowing hard, Peter got up and tiptoed across to the chair.

Tinkle! Clinkle! Plop!

There it was again! Peter took a deep breath, counted to three, then quickly pulled the chair to one side. More money fell out of his trouser pockets and plopped on to the carpet. Peter's eyes goggled! Where had all that money come from? He scooped up the money on the floor, then picked up his trousers and dug into his pockets. There was more money inside them. He counted it all very carefully. It was the exact amount of money he had paid for the Christmas crackers...

Peter sat down on his bed and stared down at

the money in his hand. What was going on? He shook his head and looked around the room hoping for some clue. Had Mum and Dad done it? Had they put the money in his pockets to make up for him losing his money in the Christmas Shop? But they didn't know exactly how much he'd paid for the crackers. And now here he was, with the exact same coins in his hand.

Then something else caught his eye. There on his bedside table, were all the Christmas cards he'd received from his friends. At the front was the card he'd got from his best friend Andy. Peter gasped and stared so hard, his eyes began to ache.

The face on the card…

Peter had seen that face before – in the Christmas Shop. The shopkeeper and Father Christmas were one and the same person… Peter picked up the card and studied it. The shopkeeper *was* Father Christmas. Peter was sure of it. And that would explain how he'd got his money back.

Which meant only one thing…

The Christmas crackers *were* magic after all.

"Thank you," Peter whispered to the Christmas card.

And he was sure that on the card, the smiling face of Father Christmas winked at him.

The Smallest Christmas Tree

Mary Dickinson

This is an adaptation of an
old North American tale.

Jason looked fiercely at the little Christmas tree sitting in a small brown flowerpot on the coffee table.

"That's too small," he said.

"It's a baby one," said Victoria. "If we look after it, it will grow into a big tree."

Jason shook his head. "I want a big tree now."

"It'll look all right when it's decorated," said Victoria. "Decorating is fun. Do you want to help?"

Jason shook his head. He folded his arms and watched. Victoria did not have fun. No matter what she did the string of fairy lights slithered off and clattered on the floor. And the branches drooped with the weight of the coloured balls, which pinged and bounced away across the floor. The tinsel stayed on but, being long, it wound round and round the tree like a bandage not a decoration.

"Oh, dear," said Victoria.

"Looks stupid," said Jason.

"What can I do?" asked Victoria.

"Get a bigger tree," said Jason.

"I can't do that, it would cost a fortune," Victoria twitched. "Oh, Grandma Taylor, what can we do?'

There was a squeaky whirring of Grandma Taylor's wheelchair as it whizzed across the front room. She thumped the brake and it wheezed to a stop in front of the coffee table.

"Jason doesn't like the Christmas tree," said Victoria. "He says it's too small."

"Too small!" repeated Grandma Taylor. "Never too small. Those decorations are too big. You need to make smaller ones."

Jason pouted his lip and shook his head. "I

want a big Christmas tree."

Grandmother Taylor looked straight into Jason's eyes. She was the same height as him in her wheelchair. "Little Christmas trees are the best," she said firmly. "Have you ever heard the story of the smallest Christmas tree?"

Jason shook his head again … and smiled. Grandma Taylor was very good at telling stories.

"It's a very old story," she said. "It's to do with how the world was made. It goes something like this…"

When the Great Creator made the world, the first things she made were the trees. Tall pointed green trees, with sides like slides and leaves like needles. She made a whole forest of them, and among all the big trees she put a very little tree. So small was this tree that all it could see were the underneath branches of the much bigger trees.

"Trees," said the Great Creator when the

evening of the first day came, "I am tired now. Could you watch over the world while I rest? For while I rest, the Great Destroyer may come and break down all I have made. You must watch out for him. Frighten him away."

"Yes, we can do that," said the trees. "We are tall. We will see him coming. We will rattle our branches and sharpen our prickles. That will scare him away."

So all through the night the trees stayed awake, even the little tree, who needed the rest. They watched for the Great Destroyer but he never came.

"Thank you," said the Great Creator in the morning.

All day long she was busy making the weather, and in the evening she came again to the trees. "Will you watch over the world while I rest?"

"Yes, yes," said the trees, and they stayed awake all night looking out for the Great Destroyer. The little tree stayed awake too. But he noticed some of the tall trees swayed in the breeze, and fell asleep, and didn't wake up till morning.

"Thank you, trees," said the Great Creator in the morning. Then she went to work making mountains and lakes, rivers and rocky deserts and lots and lots of sea.

And again in the evening she asked the trees to keep watch while she rested.

"Yes, yes," they said, but during the night many of them fell asleep.

"Wake up! Wake up!" called out the little tree. "Wake up! The Great Destroyer may come!"

"Oh, we don't all have to stay awake," yawned the big trees. "Some of us are tired. We have not slept for two whole nights."

"We must stay awake!" shouted the little tree, but his voice was drowned in the gentle swishing and swaying of sleeping trees. Luckily the Great Destroyer still did not come.

"Thank you," said the Great Creator in the morning.

During the day she made all kinds of plants, big and small, and in the evening she visited the trees again, and the trees again agreed to watch the world for her.

But almost immediately they began to fall asleep.

"No! Wake up! You mustn't!" cried the little tree. "The Great Destroyer may come. Oh, please wake up!"

The big trees grumbled, "Don't fret so, little tree! He hasn't come yet. Bet he never will." And with a sighing and a shimmering, nearly all fell to sleep.

"I'm tired, very tired," said the little Christmas tree. "But I won't fall asleep." And he didn't. With a great struggle he managed to keep himself awake till the sun rose and the day came and the Great Creator went to work once more.

That day she made animals, insects, reptiles, fishes and birds.

"Just one more night," she told the trees when

she asked them to watch the world while she slept. "Tomorrow I will make the people and then they will look after the earth. But tonight you must be extra alert for there is so much the Great Destroyer can destroy."

"Don't worry," said the trees. "We'll look after the world."

But did they? No!

The Great Creator had hardly gone when some of the trees began to sway to sleep.

"No, no!" called out the little tree. "You can't fall asleep. Wake up! Wake up!"

But they didn't wake up. As the night went on more and more trees fell asleep.

"Wake up! Wake up!" shouted the little tree.

"We're tired, tired, tired," swayed the trees.

"I'm tired too," screamed the little tree and he knew if he swayed he would soon be asleep. So he held himself straight and tall and looked this way and that for the Great Destroyer. "I am not going to fall asleep. I am not going to fall asleep," he said to himself over and over again.

The night went on. Then in the distance he thought he saw something moving.

"Did you see that?" he cried. "Did you?"

There was no reply. Every other tree was asleep.

"Wake up! Wake up!" he cried.

The big trees swayed in a helpless wave of sleep. He would have to frighten the Great Destroyer all by himself.

He held his branches out like a line of spears, every needle upright. He stretched his trunk to make himself taller and sharper.

There were slight changes in the air, slight shadows on the ground. Something was coming!

"Wake up! Wake up, trees!" His voice was thin and whispery. There was no reply.

He moved his branches rapidly up and down. Almost no sound. He rubbed them together … a small creaking sound … no more. That would scare nobody. He felt like giving up when he heard a voice he knew. It was the Great Creator.

"Thank you for looking after the world, little tree. I have my hardest job to do today so I get up early and what do I find? Only you still awake."

"We're so sorry," said the other trees, suddenly waking up. "We were so tired."

"Tired?" said the Great Creator. "And yet the youngest and smallest of you manages to stay awake. I will reward him. From now on he and all his children will be special and stay green all year, while the rest of you will lose your greenness in the winter."

And so it has been ever since...

Grandma Taylor looked at the little Christmas tree sitting in a small brown flowerpot on the coffee table.

"Our little tree is the great, great, great, millions of greats, grandchild of that first little tree. And although Christmas trees can grow very, very tall, the little ones are very, very special. Just like you."

Grandma Taylor leaned forward and gently patted Jason's cheek.

Jason jumped out of the way. He laughed. "Can I stay awake all night like the little tree? I could look out for Father Christmas."

"No," said Victoria firmly. "Us big people will do that."

"But you might fall asleep," said Jason.

"It won't matter," grinned Grandma Taylor. "He won't forget you."

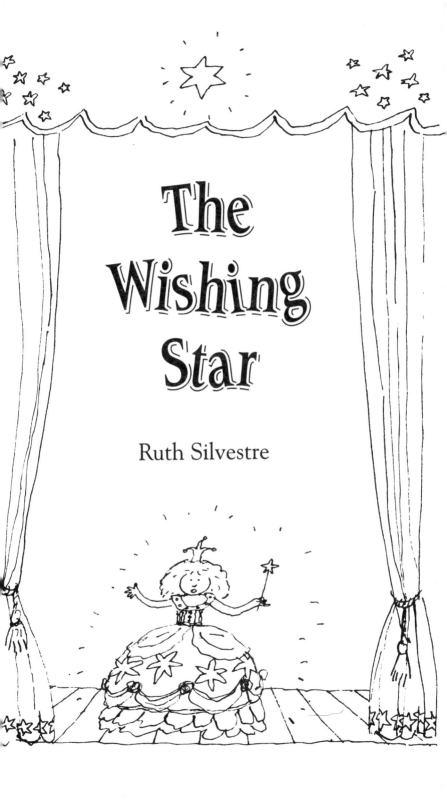

The Wishing Star

Ruth Silvestre

It was a cold December morning. The wind blew hard across the common, tearing the last leaves from the branches. Through the mini-bus window Isabella could see the ducks huddled together on the island in the middle of the pond. They looked pretty miserable too, she thought.

The other girls were laughing and chattering excitedly to each other but she just stared out through the steamy glass. She felt as though she had a heavy stone where her heart should be. And she wasn't looking forward either to telling her mum what had happened at the dancing class. She hadn't even thought about not getting into the pantomime.

After all, she had been in *Aladdin* the year

before. That had been her first time and it had been wonderful. Eight children from Tripp's dancing school had been chosen and she knew she had been one of the best. Miss Tripp herself had said so.

Isabella loved the theatre. Even when she was very little, long before she was old enough to join the dancing class, she had been to see the pantomime every year. Every year since she could remember. Her dad always took her to the matinée on Boxing Day. It was their special treat together. He understood how she loved it. He still paid for her dancing lessons.

"One day, sunshine, you'll be up there," he always said. "You've got your gran's looks." And last year she had. She had!

Her dad's mum, Isabella's gran, had been on the stage. She had died when Isabella was a baby. Her name had been Isabella too but she had called herself Bella. Bella Dawn.

When her dad and mum had split up, Dad had

given Isabella his old box full of photographs.

"I'll be moving around a lot, love," he said. "You keep them for me. Keep them safe. OK?"

Isabella loved those old photographs. Bella Dawn wore so many different costumes. There were dresses covered in spangles and lace and sometimes she was in tights and high heels and wore a silk top hat or a head-dress with tall feathers. There were pictures from every one of the shows she had been in. Her dad had kept them all.

What would he say about her not getting into the pantomime this year? She didn't know where he was but she was sure he'd turn up before Boxing Day. He always did. Like a bad penny, her mother said. The bus slowed and stopped.

" 'Bye. See you next week," they called.

Isabella waved silently, swung her bag on to her shoulder, stepped down from the minibus and crossed the road to her front gate. Her mother was in the kitchen chopping vegetables. She looked up smiling, her eyebrows raised, then shook her head sadly.

"Oh, dearie me," she said, putting down the knife and wiping her hands on her apron. "Tell me all about it then, while I make us a hot drink."

Now the tears came. The tears that Isabella had been too proud to show anyone at class. She had made herself smile and lift her chin and toss back her hair while she got dressed. She wasn't going to let them see how badly she was hurting inside.

"They only wanted six this year," she cried. "It's *Cinderella* and we're the white mice, only I'm not one of them."

"Who got chosen then?" asked her mother gently.

"Sandra and Natasha and that horrible Alice," wailed Isabella. "And ... and spotty Jennifer and beastly Barbara and stupid Sarah. They're all the same height you see and – and I'm taller. Oh, Mum, why did I have to start growing? It's not FAIR!" She put her head down on her hands and sobbed. Her mother stroked her long, fair hair.

"There, there," she said. "Have a good cry. I'm afraid you have to learn it some time, Isabella. Life isn't fair. We just have to make the best of it. Cry it all out and then forget about it."

Easy to say but jolly hard to do, Isabella thought that night as she tried to get to sleep. Her mum didn't really understand about the theatre, how important it was to her. She sighed, got out of bed and lifted down the box of photographs.

There she was: Bella Dawn, always smiling. In every picture she was smiling. She couldn't have been happy all the time, thought Isabella, no one was.

"Oh, Bella," she whispered. "This is going to be the worst Christmas I ever had."

She remembered how excited she had been the year before. The first time they had all gone on stage in the big, old theatre. At Christmas time it came alive. The rest of the year it was only used for bingo. It smelt so strange, the theatre. It smelt of old make-up and paint and glue. And there were great dark curtains at the sides of the stage that were called the wings. And everyone was so busy and you had to keep out of their way and do just as you were told.

In *Aladdin* there had been a wonderful ballet at the end of the first act. Each of the children was supposed to be a different jewel in the magic cave where Aladdin found the lamp. Isabella had been an emerald in a costume of deep, shining green. They had had to curl up very small and not move an inch until they heard Abanazar speak. Isabella could still remember the words and his really big, scary voice.

"Hold! Pause! Stop! Stay!
I'm Abanazar, villain of this play.
And now alone to work out my design
to scheme and make the magic lamp all
mine!"

Then they had to begin to move while Aladdin said:

"Why, what a gloomy place. Full of strange shadows and yet – through the darkness I seem to see a glitter of jewels."

And then as they uncurled themselves the music had started, very softly at first, then louder and the ballet had begun.

For weeks before, they had spent every Saturday morning learning the steps at dancing school. The day when they went into the dark and dusty old theatre for the first rehearsal had been exciting enough. But the first time they had gone through it in costume with the lights and music Isabella had thought she would simply burst with joy. And best of all, on Boxing Day afternoon, there in the very middle of the third row she had seen her dad. She knew he had been proud of her. If only she could have been in

Cinderella. Another tear rolled down her cheek as she put away the photographs and switched off the light.

A week later Miss Tripp called at her house.

"Isabella," she said briskly. "I know you're a sensible girl. And the best dancer I've got."

Isabella felt her face go pink and her heart begin to beat faster.

"There's a nasty bug going round the theatre," Miss Tripp went on. "And they'd feel happier if there was an understudy for the dancers – just in case one of the mice falls ill. What do you say?"

Isabella's eyes lit up. Her tummy turned right over.

"Now, don't get too excited," said Miss Tripp. "Being an understudy's a rotten job. You might not be needed at all."

But Isabella wasn't listening. Just the thought of being in the theatre was enough. At least she would be able to watch and listen.

Miss Tripp smiled. "Get your practice clothes and I'll take you down now."

Backstage at the theatre everyone was very busy. Cinderella and the Ugly Sisters were rehearsing on stage and the mice were sitting in their dressing-room.

They were surprised to see her.

"What are you doing here?" asked Jennifer, who was tying up her ballet shoes.

"We've been through our dance four times already this morning," boasted Alice.

"Look at these wonderful head-dresses we have to put on when we change into ponies," said Natasha.

"Yes," said Sarah, "and they're jolly tricky to fix on."

"Mine doesn't fit properly," wailed Barbara.

"Nonsense," said Miss Tripp, putting it firmly on Barbara's head. "Now listen to me. Isabella is going to understudy you all. Just in case any one of you catches this wretched flu."

"Natasha's been blowing her nose a lot," said Barbara.

"I have NOT!" shrieked Natasha. "I only blew it once."

"Well, Cinderella's not well," said Sarah. "She's been sneezing like anything."

"So has the Prince," said Barbara. "And Baron Hardup had to go home after lunch yesterday."

"Well – I should still go on if I was dying!" said Jennifer.

"Oh, so would I!" said Alice.

In spite of not having a part, Isabella enjoyed the next few days of rehearsals. She sat and watched every scene. At least it was better than being at home thinking about it all.

"Aren't you my little emerald from last year's *Aladdin?*" asked the director, Robin Armstrong. She nodded, pleased that he had recognized her. "Not much fun being an understudy I'm afraid," he said, "but I'll get one of the others to sit out to give you one run-through at least."

The next day Jennifer sulked as Isabella took her place in the ballet of the mice. She was pleased to find that she remembered every step. After it was finished they had to stand completely still in a half circle behind Cinderella while the Fairy Godmother spoke in a high clear voice.

"*You were kind to me when you thought I was a poor old woman,*" she said, "*but I am your Fairy Godmother and I can make your dearest wish come true.*"

She held up her magic wand and sang "When You Wish Upon a Star".

Isabella loved the song. She already knew all the words from her video of *Pinocchio*. She watched and waited for the Fairy to wave her wand and then raced off with the other mice into the wings to put on their head-dresses and change into ponies. There was a great cloud of billowing smoke from the back of the stage and on they ran again, this time pulling the beautiful golden coach. It was all very exciting. But once the rehearsal was over Jennifer took back her head-dress and Isabella had nothing to do but watch.

The Ugly Sisters made her laugh. They were men dressed up and were called Grizzle and Frizzle. And when the Prince came with the crystal slipper for them to try, one said to the other:

"Crystal slipper! You couldn't get your foot into the Crystal Palace!"

The days flew by and everyone was very kind to her. The Prince kept packets of mints in his pocket and always gave her one as he went on stage. Isabella especially liked the Fairy God-mother, whose real name was Penny Clark. She had long, fair hair like Isabella's and she was married to the pianist. They had a baby called Joey. He was six months old and Penny often had to bring him to the theatre.

Usually Joey was very good and slept most of the time but if he cried Miss Tripp would let Isabella go into the dressing-room and rock his cot and sing to him. He had fat red cheeks and a bald head with just a little quiff of blond hair on the top. Isabella loved it when he held tightly to her finger.

"How strong he is!" she said. "Look, he's trying to pull himself up."

Once, Penny let her give him his bottle and then pat his back to make him burp. Isabella enjoyed him but every single day she hoped that one of the mice would fall ill. It seemed an awful thing to wish but she did want to go on, just once.

She sat on the side of the stage, looking gloomy, as Baron Hardup, who was supposed to be Cinderella's father, finished his scene. He came and sat beside her.

"Eh up, lass," he said. "You look as though you've lost a pound and found a penny."

Isabella managed a smile. He patted her hand.

"I know," he said. "I did a bit of understudying myself. Long time ago now."

"It seems terrible to sit here wishing someone would get the flu," she sighed.

"You're really keen, aren't you?" he smiled.

Isabella nodded. "My gran was on the stage," she said. "Her name was Bella. Bella Dawn."

Baron Hardup's great black eyebrows shot up.

"Bella Dawn!" he cried. "Well, blow me down! Let's have another look at you."

He put his hand underneath her chin and turned her head from side to side. Then he nodded.

"I should have spotted it before," he said. "Well, bless me."

"Did you know my gran?" Isabella was excited.

"Did I know her? I worked with her many a time. First time must have been – oh – twenty years ago. Summer season. Blackpool. Wonderful she was. Dance like a fairy and sing like an angel, she could. Those were the good old days. Theatres there were then. All over the country."

He was still shaking his head and muttering, "Well, well, bless me," as he walked off back to his dressing-room.

By Christmas Eve not one of the mice had the flu but Penny was worried about the baby.

"He looks a bit flushed," she said. "I've been up with him half the night. Keep an eye on him for me, Isabella – there's a love."

Sure enough, as soon as his mother had gone, Joey began to cough and cry. Isabella rocked his cot. In every dressing-room there was a speaker so that you could hear what was going on on stage.

"Listen, Joey," crooned Isabella. "Listen to your mother." But Joey wailed louder. Isabella picked him up and began to walk up and down with him. He stopped crying and looked up at her. She sang to him the song his mother was singing.

"When you wish upon a star
Makes no difference who you are
Anything your heart desires will come to you."

Oh, Joey, she thought. I've been wishing and wishing but it doesn't seem to be working, does it?

On Christmas Day Isabella and her mother went to her Auntie Joan's house. She tried very hard to be cheerful. She really did love the pink sweater her mother had bought her and the velvet hat and the video of *The Nutcracker* but all the time she was wishing that just one of the mice would get the flu.

But when she got to the theatre the next day they were all as fit as fleas. Sadly she knocked on the door of Penny's dressing-room.

"Come in," someone whispered. Penny was sitting at her dressing-table with a towel over her head. She was sniffing some horrible-smelling stuff in a jug.

"Hullo, Isabella," she croaked.

"How's Joey?" asked Isabella.

"Oh, he's much better," said Penny. "My mum came down and she's got him today. But I feel awful. I don't how I'm going to get through two shows."

Robin, the director, came into the dressing-room.

"I hear our Fairy Godmother's a bit under the weather," he said.

"I'll croak my way through the lines," said Penny. "But we'll have to cut the song."

"I'm not so sure about that," said Robin, looking hard at Isabella.

Isabella's heart began to beat very fast.

"I heard someone singing your song very sweetly on Christmas Eve," he said to Penny.

"I was singing to Joey," said Isabella.

"How would you like to sing to the audience?"

Isabella swallowed. Could she? Would she dare?

"You could sing it in the wings through the microphone," he said. "Penny could mime it."

Penny looked at Isabella.

"No. It's on the stage she wants to be. I know. Let her come and stand beside me," she said. "I've got a spare costume somewhere. We can fix it with pins. What do you say, Isabella?"

And so on Boxing Day everything came right for Isabella. It was like magic, she thought. Once she stepped on to the stage into the warmth of the lights she felt at home. The conductor raised his arms, smiled up at her and the music began. She took a deep breath and sang.

"When you wish upon a star
Makes no difference who you are
Anything your heart desires will come to you
If your heart is in your dreams
No request is too extreme
When you wish upon a star as dreamers do."

And as she sang, she looked down and there he was as she knew he would be. Her dad was looking up at her. He understood. He always understood. She smiled at him as she finished the song.

"When you wish upon a star
Your dreams come true."

She bowed and smiled as the audience clapped and clapped. Her heart felt as light as a bird.

After the show everyone said how well she had sung, even the six mice. Her dad came round to the stage door to take her out to tea.

"Well, sunshine," he said. "Bella Dawn would've been proud of you. But I always said you took after her, didn't I?"

"Mmmm," said Isabella, eating her second doughnut, the jam trickling down her chin. She was surprised to find how hungry she was.

"I've got to go on again tonight," she said. "Dad –" she hesitated – "would you – would you do me a favour? Would you go and tell Mum? You see, it might be my last go. Penny might be better tomorrow."

Her father looked at her. For a moment he didn't speak, then, "Don't you worry," he said. "We'll get tickets somehow. We'll be there."

"Isn't it strange," said Isabella. "I thought this was going to be my very worst Christmas ever and…"

"Well, sunshine," he grinned. "Perhaps that's what comes of wishing on a star!"

The Last Mince Pie

Tessa Krailing

There was just one mince pie left on the plate. Barney eyed it longingly.

"Mum," he said. "Please can I –?"

"No, Barney," said Mum. "You've had quite enough already. Eat any more and you'll burst."

"But there's only one left," he pointed out. "It looks sort of lonely sitting there all by itself."

"*No*, Barney!"

He sighed. It was true he had already eaten rather a lot, but after all it was Christmas. At Christmas you're supposed to eat a lot. Everybody does. Grandad had tucked into the roast potatoes, which he said were "truly scrumdumptious", and Dad had had two big helpings of Christmas pudding and custard. Even Alice, his younger sister, who was very picky with her food, had eaten twice as much as usual.

As for Barney, he had had two helpings of *everything*. Turkey, ham, crispy bacon rolls, chipolata sausages, chestnut stuffing, potatoes, peas, gravy and cranberry sauce. Followed by Christmas pudding and two mince pies. Mince pies were his absolute favourite, especially the ones Mum made, which had golden puff pastry outside and lots of rich mincemeat inside and a frosting of sugar on top. Oh, they were what Grandad would call scrumdumptious! The best food ever invented.

And there was just one left on the plate...

Perhaps, if he reached out his hand when nobody was looking, he could grab it and stuff it into his jeans pocket, then make some excuse to rush up to his room and eat it in secret. The pastry might get a bit crumbly on the way but that wouldn't matter. It would still taste as good. His mouth watered at the thought.

But then he caught Grandad's eye.

"I wouldn't if I were you," Grandad warned. "Always leave the last mince pie for the Christmas Beastie, that's my advice. If you don't it can lead to trouble."

"What's the Christmas Beastie?" asked Barney.

Grandad looked surprised. "Haven't I ever told you the story of the Christmas Beastie?"

"No, you haven't," said Alice. "Go on, Grandad. Tell us now."

But Mum said, "I don't think you'd like it, Alice. It's rather a scary story and might give you bad dreams. It certainly gave *me* bad dreams when I was a child."

"Did it?" said Grandad, looking even more surprised. "Oh, well, in that case I'd better zip up my mouth." He pretended to fasten his lips together with a zipping noise.

"Oh, Grandad, please tell us," begged Alice, who loved scary stories. "I won't have bad dreams. I never have bad dreams. Tell us about the Christmas Beastie."

"Yes, tell us," said Barney, who wanted to know why not leaving the last mince pie should lead to trouble. Not that it would put him off wanting to eat it.

Grandad shook his head, his lips still fastened tightly together.

Mum sighed. "Oh, very well," she said. "But take them into the other room and tell the story there, while I make some coffee."

"And I'll clear the table." Dad started to pile up the empty dishes.

Grandad pretended to unzip his lips. "Come on, kids," he said, pushing back his chair. "Let's go and sit by the fire. That's the best place to tell a story."

Alice jumped to her feet and followed him through the archway that led into the sitting-room.

Reluctantly Barney stood up. His jeans seemed to have got very tight around his middle, but even though he felt so full he was sure he still had a small space left in his stomach for the last mince pie. He stood staring at it...

"Barney!" Grandad called from the sitting-room.

"I'm coming." He cast a last, longing look over his shoulder as he left the table.

Grandad was already seated in the armchair, lighting up his pipe. A log fire roared in the grate and Alice sat on the rug. "Hurry up, Barney," she said. "I can't wait to hear about the Christmas Beastie."

Barney slumped on the sofa. He hoped the story wouldn't go on too long. Some of Grandad's stories went on for ages. Grandad was old – about fifty at least – and when he was in the Merchant Navy he had sailed around the world several times. He had been shipwrecked twice. The first time he was nearly swallowed by a whale and the second time he was saved by a mermaid. That's why he had such blue eyes, Mum said, because he had spent so much time gazing at the sea.

His eyes were very blue now, as he sat in the chair beside the fire, and he seemed in no great hurry to start.

"Go on," Alice prompted. "We're listening."

Grandad puffed on his pipe. "Well," he began, "the Christmas Beastie lives in a cave high up in the mountains…"

"What mountains?" Barney interrupted. "There aren't any mountains round here."

"Oh, yes, there are," said Grandad. "But only at this time of year. That's why they're called the Christmas Mountains."

"Where do they go the rest of the year?"

Grandad shrugged. "Who knows? All I can tell you is that they're very high and the peaks are covered with white icing, like a Christmas cake. And they are full of deep, dark caves."

"And that's where the Beastie lives," said Alice, who was impatient to get on with the story.

"Yes, that's where the Beastie lives. Or rather sleeps. All the year round he sleeps, until about eleven o'clock on Christmas morning, when he gets his first whiff of roasting turkey. That's when he lifts up his head and has a good sniff." Grandad removed the pipe from his mouth and gave several loud sniffs. "'Ho, hum!' he says. 'I can smell something scrumdumptious a-cooking down below!' And he gets up and has a jolly good stretch and then goes outside his cave to take a shufti."

"What's a shufti?" asked Barney.

"A good look round. And what do you think he sees?"

"Christmas trees," said Alice. "And holly and mistletoe and paper chains and silver bells." She glanced at the fire. "And smoke coming out of chimneys."

"All those things," agreed Grandad. "But the Beastie isn't really interested in trees and holly and whatnot. He's only interested in FOOD! That's what he can smell and that's what he's after. So off he goes, shambling down the mountainside like some big old bear, in search of a house where they're cooking up a grand feast, just like the one we've been eating."

"Is that what he looks like?" asked Barney. "A bear?"

"Oh, no. No, he doesn't look anything like a bear. He doesn't look anything like anything, really. That's why he's so hard to spot."

"Do you mean he's invisible?" asked Alice.

"Sort of," said Grandad. "Unless you know what you're looking for. Then you can usually spot him straight away."

"Why, what are you looking for?" asked Barney.

"Rubbish," said Grandad. "The sort of stuff that was lying around this morning after you'd undone your presents. Bows and ribbon and labels and sticky-tape, the wrapping paper you tore off in little bits because you were in such a hurry to get them open. That sort of thing. That's what he looks like."

Alice glanced a little nervously at the wastepaper basket, which was still piled high with Christmas rubbish. "You mean ... like that?" she said, pointing.

Grandad nodded. "Exactly like that. Which is why nobody notices him. He can hang around in corners for days sometimes, without anyone knowing he's there. Because he won't leave, you see, until he's eaten the last mince pie."

Barney stared at his grandfather. "The last mince pie?"

"Aye, that's why I warned you not to take it. As long as he gets that last mince pie he's happy. He's ready to go then, back to his cave in the Christmas Mountains, where he'll fall asleep and not wake up for another year."

"But what – what if he doesn't get it?" asked Barney. "What if somebody else eats it first?"

"Ah." Grandad's eyes grew bluer than the deepest ocean. "Well, then something terrible happens. Something really shocking."

"What? What?" asked Alice impatiently.

He shook his head. "It's too terrible even to talk about."

"Oh, *Grandad!*" groaned Barney and Alice together.

At that moment Mum came into the room, carrying a tray of coffee. "Story-telling finished?" she asked.

"Pretty well," said Grandad.

"No, it isn't!" said Alice. "He won't tell us what happens if the Christmas Beastie doesn't get the last mince pie."

"Do you know, Mum?" asked Barney.

"No, I don't," she said. "Because I was never greedy enough to take it. Now, is there anything good on television?"

At once everyone started arguing about which programmes they wanted to watch and forgot all about the Christmas Beastie.

Except Barney, that is. He couldn't stop thinking about the last mince pie. Was it still there, sitting on the plate, or had Dad put it away in the tin when he was clearing the table? Or – horrors! – had he sneakily eaten it himself while nobody was looking?

Later that afternoon, when the grown-ups had fallen asleep and Alice was reading her new dinosaur book, Barney quietly went to look through the archway into the dining-room. All the dirty dishes had gone except one. The plate with the mince pie still sat amidst the mats and the pulled crackers and the screwed-up paper napkins. Had Dad left it there because he thought someone might fancy it for supper? Or had he just forgotten about it?

Barney was tempted. He was very, very tempted. After all, if it disappeared people would only think that the Christmas Beastie had taken it. No one would suspect him. But then, in his mind, he heard Grandad's voice:

"*...something terrible happens. Something really shocking.*"

He decided to wait until supper. Then Mum

would surely ask if anyone would like to finish up the leftovers. And he would say, "Yes, please. I'll have the mince pie," and she would say, "Here you are then, since nobody else seems to want it." That way no one could accuse him of being greedy. He went back to sit on the sofa.

But at supper Mum said nothing about the last mince pie and Barney didn't like to mention it in case Grandad started talking about the Beastie again.

Soon it was time for bed.

Alice went first. As she kissed Grandad good night she whispered, "Don't worry, I shan't have bad dreams."

"Of course you won't," he said. "You've nothing to fear from the Christmas Beastie."

She went happily upstairs to bed.

Barney put off going as long as he could, even though he was finding it hard to keep his eyes open. But eventually Mum insisted it was time, so he said good night and reluctantly left the room. On his way out he glanced through the archway into the dining-room.

Yes, it was still there, looking just as scrumdumptious as ever.

Again Barney was tempted. He was very, very tempted. But he was afraid that if he tried to grab it from the plate someone might see him. So he left it and went to bed.

About an hour later he heard Grandad come upstairs, and then Mum and finally Dad. At last the house was silent. But although Barney was tired he couldn't sleep. He kept thinking and thinking of that last mince pie, still lying on the plate in the dining-room. Mum must have forgotten about it. They had all forgotten about it. By morning it would be stale. What a waste of a mince pie!

He flung back the quilt and crept stealthily downstairs to the dining-room. It was very dark, but he dared not put on the main light. Instead he groped his way along the wall until he found the switch for the Christmas tree. Perfect! The tree stood in the archway between the living-room and the dining-room, and its coloured lights were just bright enough for him to see that the mince pie was still there, just begging to be eaten.

Barney stared at it. Of course he didn't believe Grandad's story, any more than he believed his other stories about whales and mermaids. There was no such thing as the Christmas Beastie. Besides, if nobody ever ate the last mince pie that meant there must be hundreds of last mince pies – thousands, millions, billions, trillions of last mince pies – lying around on plates all over the world. The Christmas Beastie couldn't eat them all. No, it was just a story grown-ups told to stop children being greedy. Typical! He reached out his hand.

"Something terrible happens … too terrible even to talk about."

But grown-ups only say that when they can't think of a good ending to the story. Of course nothing terrible would happen. He, Barney, was too old to be taken in by that kind of nonsense. He grabbed the mince pie, stuffed it into his mouth and gobbled it down. Oh, but it was scrumdumptious! Flaky and crumbly and sweet and satisfying.

He wiped his mouth on the back of his hand and laughed to himself. "Bad luck, Beastie!" he muttered. "I beat you to it."

What was that noise?

He looked round quickly, but there was no one in the room except himself. Then he heard it again, a faint, rustling sound. It seemed to be coming from the wastepaper basket, which was still piled high with crumpled wrapping paper from this morning. Could it be a mouse? Cautiously Barney crept nearer.

There it was again! He couldn't see very clearly in the light coming from the Christmas tree, but it looked as if the wrapping paper had begun to move about. It *must* be a mouse. Then he noticed that some tinsel had become attached to his sleeve and tried to brush it off, but it seemed to be stuck. At the same moment bits of paper came flying out of the wastepaper basket towards him as if drawn by a magnet, followed by bows and ribbons and gift tags. Next came some pine needles lying beneath the Christmas tree, and then more tinsel and baubles and cotton wool snow, until eventually he was covered in bits of paper and decorations.

Then everything in the room went red.

Puzzled, Barney turned round and round in a circle, but everywhere he looked was lit by a deep red glow. Suddenly he caught sight of his reflection in the mirror over the mantelshelf. At least he supposed it was his reflection. All he could see was a mountainous heap of rubbish, like some huge tatty monster, and at the top, where his eyes should be, were two red Christmas tree lights, flashing and glowing in the dark. Too late he realized what Grandad had been trying to warn him about. Now he knew what happened if you ate the last mince pie…

You turn into the Christmas Beastie!

No, that was silly. He must be having a bad dream. Yes, that was it. Mum had warned them about the bad dreams. Any minute now he would wake up and find himself in bed.

But where *was* his bed?

Strangely, he couldn't quite remember. Everything seemed to have gone very misty and confused. Where was he? Where was this place? It looked like somebody's home, but it wasn't his. He didn't belong here. He had a much better home than this, somewhere warmer and darker…

Oh, yes … now he remembered. His bed was in that cave in the mountains. That warm, dark cave where he could sleep and sleep for another whole year, until the feasting began again. His cave high up in the icing-covered Christmas Mountains. Slowly he began to slither and rustle and shamble out of the dining-room, through the hall and towards the back door…

Next morning at breakfast Mum asked, "Where's Barney?"

"I don't think he's awake yet," said Alice. "I haven't heard a sound from his room."

"I'll go and give him a shout," said Dad. He went upstairs.

When he came down again he said, "That's strange. He seems to have disappeared. I've looked all over the place but there's no sign of him."

"Where on earth can he be?" said Mum.

Grandad sighed. "Haven't you noticed anything?"

"Yes," said Alice. "Somebody's tidied up."

"So they have!" said Mum, looking through the archway. "What an extraordinary thing!"

"That's not all," said Grandad. "Does anyone know what happened to the last mince pie?"

"Somebody must have eaten it," said Dad. "I

forgot to put it away last night and didn't re-member until I was upstairs in bed. But when I came down first thing this morning it had gone."

Mum looked at Grandad. "What does it mean?"

"I'm afraid," he said gravely, "it means that the worst has happened. I very much doubt if we shall see Barney again until this time next year – and then only if he can find someone else greedy enough to eat the last mince pie."

Meanwhile, from a warm, dark cave high up in the Christmas Mountains came the sound of snoring – and the occasional satisfied belch.

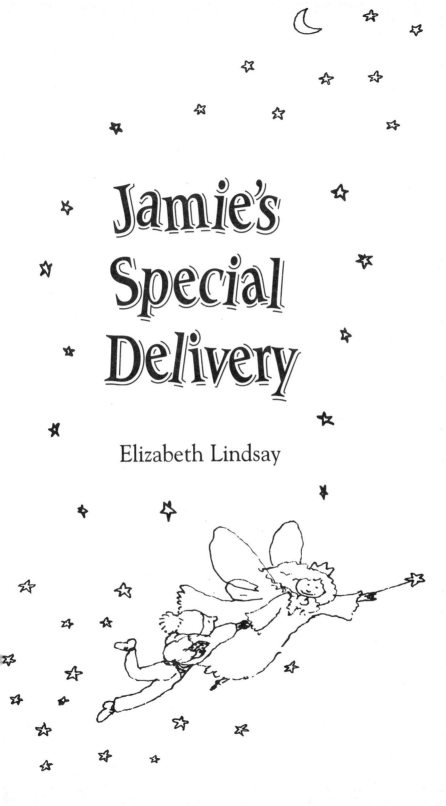

Jamie's Special Delivery

Elizabeth Lindsay

Yelling plumes of steamy breath, the three MacDougal children ran up the frosty path to the warmth of the open front door. Sandie and Roy shoved past Jamie just as one of the handles on his carrier bag snapped.

"Pushy twins," Jamie grumbled, struggling to save his precious shopping.

Dad arrived with a box of groceries and Jamie's bag spilled over the doormat. There was a horrid crunch as Dad's foot landed on a box of muesli bars – Sandie's Christmas present. Jamie stared in horror.

"Don't worry. The crumbs'll taste as good as whole bars," said Dad. "The box'll straighten out. Sandie won't mind." But Jamie minded. Tears crept into his eyes.

"Whatever's the matter?" asked Mum, coming downstairs.

"An accident," said Dad as he carried his groceries to the kitchen.

Mum bent down beside Jamie and picked up the squashed box. She squeezed and moulded until it looked less crumpled.

"Will that do?"

"I suppose so," said Jamie. Mum turned to the other things scattered across the mat.

"You're not to look," said Jamie. "One of these is for you." Mum held the torn carrier open and closed her eyes.

"I'll hold, you fill," she said. "Then I want you to get your coat off and help me get the Christmas decorations down from the attic."

"But what about my presents?" said Jamie. "Someone might look."

"We'll find a secret place in your bedroom."

They were halfway up the stairs when the telephone rang.

"Can you get it, Bob," Mum called.

Dad ran from the kitchen and grabbed the receiver.

"What! Oh, no!" he was heard to say before they disappeared into Jamie's bedroom.

"Under the bed?" suggested Mum.

"Under my duvet," said Jamie.

"OK," said Mum, swinging the tattered bag on to the top of a pair of bunk beds. "I'll leave you to do the hiding." And she hurried away to find out who was on the phone.

Dumping his coat on the floor, Jamie climbed to the top bunk and wriggled under the duvet, pulling his secret hoard with him. He made a tunnel to let in the light and tipped the carrier upside down.

Jamie rattled the muesli bars in their battered box and shrugged, deciding that Dad was probably right, Sandie wouldn't mind crumbs. He sniffed the tablet of rose soap for Mum and wrinkled his nose. Very whiffy. He put it next to the pile of liquorice shoelaces he'd bought for Dad, none of which, he promised himself, was he going to eat. A paper bag held four pink sugar mice for Roy. Easy to leave *them*. They were yuk! For Bella a special large doggy shoe chew. Jamie guessed by the scratching and whining at the door she had already smelt it. Tough. She wasn't getting it until Christmas Day.

Putting the chew to one side, Jamie picked up a weighty silver tin. He ran his finger over the bumpy blue lettering. This was his prize present. He'd searched for ages, dragging his impatient Dad up and down the High Street until he'd seen the tin winking at him from a shelf at the back of a poky little knick-knack shop. This was Granny MacDougal's Christmas present – a tin of Old Fashioned Treacle Toffee. Her favourite! He was longing to see her face when she opened it. Although it seemed like for ever, Granny would be with them by teatime. He could hardly wait.

Jamie quickly piled the presents back in the

carrier and crawled out of his tunnel, squashing the duvet behind him. He jumped to the floor, squeezed through his bedroom door to keep Bella out and made his way downstairs.

Four gloomy faces looked up at him from the hall.

"What's up?" asked Jamie.

"Come in the kitchen, old lad," said Dad. "Bad news, I'm afraid."

"It's Gran," said Roy. "She's not coming."

"She is," said Jamie, rushing after his parents. "She is coming!"

"No," said Dad. "She can't come now. She slipped on some ice and sprained her ankle."

"But why should that stop her?" said Jamie.

"She's not allowed to walk for a few days," explained Mum. "Her ankle has to be rested so it can get better."

"At least she didn't break it," said Sandie. "Then she'd have been in plaster. She might have got cut open and had metal plates nailed in."

"Gross," said Roy. "Do you have to?"

"I'm saying it was good she didn't."

"Yes, it is," said Mum. "But it's very disappointing she can't come for Christmas."

"But where will she go?" asked Jamie. "Who's going to look after her?"

"She's at Uncle Pete and Auntie Ellen's," said Dad. "I've just spoken to her on the phone and she says she's fine, being waited on hand and foot, and only sorry that such a silly thing happened."

"But what about her Christmas presents," wailed Jamie. "What about that?"

"It's too late to put them in the post so we're all going up to Uncle Pete's for Hogmanay. We'll give them to her then," said Mum.

Jamie sat on the nearest chair and scowled with disappointment. Christmas Day was tomorrow. How could this happen when he'd got Granny the best present ever? He sighed a big sigh and slumped across the table with his chin in his hands.

"It's tough," said Dad, patting his shoulder. "I know how you feel."

"It's no good being miserable," said Mum, "although I know we all are. We're going to have to make the best of it. And we still haven't decorated the tree. Let's fetch the decorations from the attic."

The attic, where Mum and Dad slept, had a cubby hole at the far end. Inside this cramped and cluttered room, Mum, on hands and knees, tugged at a box.

"It's the Christmas tree lights," said Sandie.

"Ask Dad to carry it down," said Mum. "There should be another box."

From his pocket Jamie took out a small torch and crawled into the cubby hole beside his mother.

"Oh, good, Jamie, shine it on this," said Mum. There was the crinkle of tissue paper and the shimmer of a silver ball. "That's the one," said Mum. "We've found it."

Downstairs Dad and Roy busied themselves untangling the Christmas lights while Sandie and Jamie unwrapped the decorations, covering the floor with tissue paper. They quickly made a pile of silver balls, golden stars and glittering tinsel and Sandie was soon helping Mum arrange things on the tree.

"We should have done this days ago," said Mum, "if a certain person had brought the tree home." Dad said nothing. It was a sore point that he'd forgotten twice to collect it.

Jamie rummaged right down to the bottom of the decorations box where he found a grubby cardboard container. He lifted it out. Inside was something wrapped in ancient tissue paper. Soon he found himself holding a tattered, worn little doll. It took Jamie a moment or two to realize what it was.

"A fairy," he exclaimed. "A Christmas tree fairy to go on top of the tree."

"Not that old thing," said Sandie. "What about

my special silver star? Mum said I could put that on top. You did say, didn't you, Mum?"

"That old fairy's seen better days, Jamie," said Dad. "She's a bit faded and old-fashioned for our tree. She's not been out of her box for years. I'm surprised we've still got her." Somewhat regretfully, Jamie wrapped the fairy up. "She's the Christmas fairy I had when I was a boy," continued Dad. "And she was old then. She belonged to Granny when she was a girl."

"To Granny!" said Jamie, unwrapping the fairy again. He looked at her more closely. She was old, with faded golden hair and a tarnished silver crown. She held a dull silver wand with a star on it and wore a grey-brown dress which once must have been white. When you moved her on to her back her eyes closed and when she was upright they opened again.

"Granny's fairy," Jamie whispered. "Can I take her up to my room?" he asked. "If no one minds." He wanted someone to talk to about Granny's

Christmas present and Granny's Christmas fairy would certainly do.

"No, no one minds," said Mum.

"And can I have some wrapping paper and some sticky tape?"

"Paper and sticky tape are in the bag underneath the book shelves," said Mum.

Grinning, Jamie wrapped the fairy up in her tissue paper and put her back in her box. He chose three sheets of wrapping paper and searched for the sticky tape. Then, gathering everything up, he set off upstairs. Bella gambolled past him, glad to be let into the living-room at last. Cries of "Who let the dog in?" followed Jamie upstairs as Bella ran off with the tinsel.

Back in his room Jamie put the paper and sticky tape on his table and the fairy box on the floor. Unwrapping her carefully he laid the fairy on the clean duvet covering the bottom bunk. Granny's bed. The fairy lay with eyes closed. The thought of Granny's cancelled visit gave Jamie such a sad feeling that it almost hurt. Quickly he cleared a pile of comics off the mantelpiece and moved his tyrannosaurus rex to the book shelf. He lifted the fairy up. She opened her eyes and looked straight at him. Jamie smiled.

"Hello, Granny's fairy. I'm going to put you on the mantelpiece so you can see everything that's going on." The fairy couldn't sit as her legs wouldn't bend so Jamie propped her upright between two piles of books.

"There," he said. "Now you can watch me wrap my presents."

He climbed to the top bunk and pulled the carrier bag from its hiding place. He arranged the presents on the floor in a line. Muesli bars, sugar mice, soap, liquorice shoe-laces, doggy shoe chew and Old Fashioned Treacle Toffee.

"See," he said to the fairy. "Nice presents. Only Granny can't come now. The toffee's for her and I wanted her to have it on Christmas Day. I would ask Father Christmas to do a special delivery but

I don't know how to get hold of him." The fairy blinked. Jamie gave her a long stare then laughed at himself. He'd imagined it, of course.

"I'm going to wrap my presents now," he said, "and later put them round the Christmas tree. But only when Bella's not around. She'd eat the lot. Even Mum's soap. She ate some soap once so I know."

The wrapping up was fiddly and took a long time. So did writing out the labels, cutting them out and sticking them on. But when he had finished he was really pleased. The presents were a mystery now. No finding out what they were until Christmas Day. Only he and the fairy knew. He bundled them into the carrier bag – all except Granny's, which he put on the books next to the fairy.

"I want you to look after that one," he said. "Keep it safe for Granny." Out of the corner of his eye he pretended he saw the fairy nod. Jamie touched her head.

"I wish you could nod. But you can't, can you? Your head doesn't move one little bit." And he picked up his carrier bag and went downstairs.

By bedtime Jamie had got used to the idea that Granny wasn't coming. He was thinking more about the letter he had written to Father Christmas asking for a sledge. He pulled back the curtains and looked outside. Jamie needed snow. A sledge without snow was no use at all. The night was full of stars and a round moon sent shimmering, silver light across the rooftops. Jamie touched the chill glass and shivered. It was very cold.

"If some clouds did come, then it might snow," he said, climbing to his top bunk. He snuggled under the duvet as Mum came in to read him a story. But he couldn't concentrate.

"Mum, you will make sure Bella doesn't eat Father Christmas's mince pies or knock over his sherry, won't you?"

"I will," promised Mum. Jamie was still smarting

from Roy's comments about Dad eating the mince pies and drinking the sherry because there was no such person as Father Christmas. For Jamie the idea of a sleigh gliding through the sky drawn by magic reindeer was thrilling. He knew too, that when Father Christmas delivered their Christmas stockings he would be glad of a snack and a wee dram. *Wee dram*, that's what Granny MacDougal always called Santa's Christmas sherry.

"I wish Granny was here."

"I know you do," said Mum, brushing the hair out of his eyes. "So do I. But we'll see her for Hogmanay. That'll be nice, won't it?"

"Not as nice as having her here now."

"No, not as nice as that." Mum kissed him good night and switched out the light.

Moonlight spilled through a crack in the curtains, lighting up the fairy on the mantelpiece.

"I wish…" said Jamie. "I wish you could talk and fly and magic me to Uncle Pete's with

Granny's present. I wish you could." He stared at the moonlit fairy and the fairy stared back. Then slowly, slowly, without his meaning them to, Jamie's eyes closed.

They opened again abruptly. Yet Jamie didn't know whether he was asleep or awake. It was dark and yet it wasn't. A silver light glowed at the end of the bed. Jamie sat up. The light moved and the room was full of flickering shadows. The brightness danced towards him down the duvet. It was a tiny girl, with sparkling, golden hair and a shimmering white dress. Jamie was dazzled by her silver crown and glittering wand.

"It's you," said Jamie. "You're the Christmas tree fairy." The room filled with the tinkling of bells as the fairy laughed. On the mantelpiece, where the fairy should have been, was an empty space.

"One wish," said the fairy. "And you've already made it."

"Have I?" said Jamie. The fairy pointed her

wand at Granny's Christmas present. The present glided from the mantelpiece to land beside Jamie on the duvet.

"That's magic!" said Jamie, hardly believing his eyes.

"It's time to go," said the fairy. Jamie climbed from his bunk. The fairy fluttered her wings, sending a powder of twinkling stars to cover his hair. In a trice Jamie was wearing all his clothes, including his warm anorak and woolly hat. He was extremely surprised.

"Don't forget your granny's present," said the fairy. "Hold my hand and don't let go."

Full of wonder, Jamie picked up the present and took hold of the fairy's hand. Her tiny fingers gripped his and, with a wave of her wand, the curtains drew back and the window opened. Together they flew high into the air – towards the moon, shedding her pale light, and towards the stars.

Orange lights flickered on the cold earth,

where rooftops and streets, fields and hills, lay far below under a white hoar frost. Laughing with delight, Jamie held tight to the fairy. This was the most exciting journey of his life.

In what seemed like no time at all they fell from the sky. Down and down they came, past a rooftop and a bedroom, to a window which opened in welcome. In they went, lighting the room with silver. A ginger bundle asleep on the sofa didn't so much as stir. Jamie recognized Winston, Uncle Pete's and Auntie Ellen's cat. Around a small tinselled tree was a cluster of parcels. Jamie placed Granny's on top of the pile, not once letting go of the fairy's hand. She put a finger to her lips and smiled. Jamie smiled back, imagining how surprised Granny would be in the morning.

Then they were outside again and the window closed behind them, tucking the house up as before. They sped home past millions of stars, slipping from the sky to fly in through Jamie's open window. Before he knew it, Jamie was sitting up in bed in his pyjamas and the silver light was fading.

"Thank you very much," he whispered, snuggling under the duvet. "Good night, Christmas tree fairy." A peal of bells trilled with the fairy's faint "Good night". In spite of all his efforts not to let them, Jamie's eyes closed.

When next he woke, daylight had crept under the curtains. On the mantelpiece, in the half light, he could just make out the Christmas tree fairy propped between the two piles of books as if nothing had happened. At the bottom of his bed hung a stocking and underneath the stocking was what looked like a very large parcel.

"It's Christmas," cried Jamie, sliding out of bed. With the curtains back he could see everything properly. It *was* a large parcel. The label said "To Jamie, Happy Christmas, With love from Mum and Dad". He ripped paper madly to find a wooden seat and runners. It was a sledge. He rushed back to the window. The sky was hung with heavy grey clouds and a robin, its red breast fluffed against the chill, pecked cold crumbs from the bird table. When Jamie opened the window there was a stillness as though everything waited.

"Please, let it snow. Please, please," he begged before closing the window against the cold and returning to his wonderful sledge.

The door burst open and the twins rushed in.

"What did you get?" Sandie wanted to know. "We got bikes!"

"Actually in our bedrooms," said Roy.

"A sledge just like I wanted," cried Jamie. "Look!"

It was at breakfast that the row happened. Jamie couldn't keep quiet any longer and told the twins he had delivered Granny MacDougal's Christmas present.

"Don't be pea-brained," said Roy. "Fly through the air. You must think we're loop heads."

"I did. I went in the night. It was magic."

"More like a dream," said Sandie.

"Well, where is it then? Where's the present?"

"You've hidden it," said Roy.

"No, I haven't. It's not there," said Jamie. "You see if you can find it. You never can."

"Now, that's enough," said Mum. "It's a lovely thought, Jamie. But, well…"

"I did. I went with the Christmas tree fairy. I did."

Mum smiled. "Come on," she said. "Everyone finished? There's Christmas stockings to open and presents from under the tree."

Jamie was so angry he went stomping upstairs and slammed his bedroom door as hard as he could. He sat in the middle of the floor and fumed.

"Why can't you tell them?" he said, looking up at the fairy. The fairy stared straight above his head. She didn't look a bit magic now, just old and faded and worn. "We did go, didn't we?"

Bella scrabbled at the door. Jamie let her in and she trotted to the mantelpiece. Stretching up, she tried to sniff the fairy. Her nose didn't quite reach. She slid to the floor and snuffled Jamie instead, licking his ears and neck while he shouted "help" and "gerroff". He rolled around the carpet with Bella tumbling after him.

"We did deliver it," cried Jamie. "Because I know for a fact that Granny's treacle toffee is not in this house and it's not in your tummy either, Bella, because you couldn't reach." And that's how Mum found the pair of them. In a heap.

It was after the biggest Christmas dinner in the world, when they were lying in front of the telly watching a video, that the phone rang. Dad heaved himself up to answer it.

"It's Granny," he said. At which everyone got interested and Mum switched off the video. "She wants to speak to Jamie." Dad raised his eyebrows as if he couldn't quite believe what he was about to say. "To thank him for the Christmas present!" Mum and the twins just stared.

"Oh, good," said Jamie. "Then she must like it." Drifting white flakes drew his eye to the window. "And," he cried, "it's starting to snow!" With a whoop he rushed to tell Granny everything, leaving the rest of his family gaping with astonishment.

The
Christmas
Shawl

Sue Stops

Nobody knew more about knitting than Agatha. She understood the most complicated patterns and her fingers seemed to fly. She knitted Fair Isle jumpers for sportsmen, colourful jumpers for children, long scarves, warm mittens and soft toys. Any bits of wool left over were knitted into squares and made into bright blankets for people in countries far away.

Best of all Agatha liked knitting shawls – soft, white lacy ones for happy mothers to wrap around newly born babies. All her friends' children and their children's children received a new shawl when a baby was born. Agatha's shawls were cherished and instead of finishing up in a jumble sale were put away in bottom drawers for another time.

Agatha's granddaughter Becky was six. She loved watching her grandmother's fingers as they knitted coloured balls of wool into clothes fit for a king.

"I'd like to learn to knit," said Becky one day. Her granny smiled.

"I'd better teach you," she said, reaching into her long needle case for a special pair she knew were there. "A long time ago my grandmother taught me to knit with these," she laughed. "Now it's my turn to do the same.

"It takes patience to learn how to knit. Through the stitch, loop the wool, pull it through and off," she said, over and over again. Becky struggled, got angry with herself but stuck at it. The first piece of knitting she cast off looked like a piece of old fishing net but Agatha didn't laugh.

"You must treasure it," she said. "Wrap it in tissue paper and one day you can show it to your granddaughter and tell her how your granny taught you to knit. Of course, it might be your grandson – some of the best knitters in the world are men!"

Becky got quite good at knitting, but more exciting things were happening. Christmas was coming and school became quite the most exciting place to be in all the world. There were secret cards and presents to be made. A huge decorated tree was put up in the hall and the children learnt carols to sing during the Nativity play which they always performed in the church for their parents.

Mrs Barnes, their teacher, reached down the Christmas box from the top of a tall cupboard and produced costumes for everyone to wear. There was a blue gown for Mary; tea-towel head-dresses for the shepherds, golden cardboard crowns for the kings and white muslin dresses with tinsel haloes for the angels. She collected baby Jesus from a cupboard in the hall where he was stored in straw in an old wooden tomato-box manger.

Becky was worried about Jesus. He was just an old doll, wrapped in what looked like bandages. Mrs Barnes explained that they were swaddling bands. "It's the way they wrapped up newborn babies in the times when Jesus lived. It's in the Christmas story," she told the children.

"I think baby Jesus should wear special clothes," Becky said to her granny when she got home. "I'm sure he'll be all right," Agatha reassured her.

The day before they performed the play for their parents in the church, the children went there for a special rehearsal. All the props were taken – the lanterns, animal masks, costumes and baby Jesus in his manger. While they were rehearsing it started to snow.

"That's all we need," groaned Mrs Barnes, who hated the stuff, but of course the children got very excited. "Let's hope it clears up by tomorrow – it's so messy!" But it didn't. It got much colder and very frosty.

"It's too cold to snow any more," remarked Agatha as Becky snuggled up close by the fire with her. Granny was babysitting, and knitting away at another shawl. Becky was unusually quiet.

"Penny for your thoughts," said Agatha, breaking the silence.

"I'm thinking about baby Jesus in his manger," answered Becky. "He's going to be very cold tonight when they put off the heating in the church. Those swaddling bands won't be much use!"

"Granny," said Becky after another long thoughtful silence. "Granny – please could we wrap him up in one of your shawls just to be sure that he's warm enough?"

Agatha laughed again. "Becky, it's much too dangerous to go out when it's dark and frosty. We might slip." She stopped, sensed an excitement she couldn't resist, and changed her mind. "All right," she agreed. "I've nearly finished this one. I'll just cast off, then we'll take it round to the church and wrap him up."

Quickly she put the finishing touches to the shawl, carefully wrapped it up and put it into a plastic bag. Then they both put on their warmest clothes, and set off, hand in hand. It wasn't easy, but Becky loved the snow.

They arrived at the church just as the choir was leaving after their practice. The Choirmaster jangled the keys to hurry the last boy from the church. He looked at Agatha and the little girl.

"You can't go in," he said. "I'm just locking up."

"Oh, dear," said Agatha sadly. "What a pity." She smiled. "We've just brought something along ready for the children's play tomorrow."

"Oh, all right then," said the Choirmaster, weakening. "I'll hang on for just a couple of minutes." He switched on the light which had been specially placed over the manger, to shine like a star.

He watched as the old lady and little girl walked slowly up the aisle, gazing round the church at mysterious places where the light didn't reach.

He watched as they reached the manger and leaned over. He saw Becky lift the doll and wrap it in the wondrously white lacy shawl she took from a bag. It seemed to shimmer in the light. He smiled as Becky kissed the doll before she laid it gently back in the manger, then hugged her grandmother. They both looked specially happy as they walked back to the door.

"Thank you for waiting," said Agatha to the Choirmaster and Becky added, "He'll be all right now."

The Choirmaster locked the door behind them, glad to have helped something rather special happen. "Merry Christmas!" he called after them, smiling.

*   *   *

Next day the play was set to be an enormous success. Agatha was there with Becky's mum who had got time off work, and they watched proudly as Becky, dressed as an angel, stood quietly in her place. One thing nearly spoilt the day. At the back of the church a baby cried and cried. It threatened to stop the performance because no one could hear what the children were saying or singing. Some parents started "tut-tutting" and glared round at the embarrassed mother. Becky was very sorry for the little baby and when she heard what one of the mothers sitting at the front was whispering to her friend, she decided to take matters into her own hands.

"Poor little thing – I expect it's feeling the cold," she heard the lady say. Becky listened to the baby, looked at baby Jesus snug and warm in his manger and knew just what to do.

She clambered down from the bench where she was standing, and walked across to the manger.

"What are you doing?" hissed Mrs Barnes, under her breath. "Becky – go back to your place." But Becky was determined.

She carefully took the white lacy shawl from baby Jesus and tucked him back deep into the straw. Then she carried the shawl to the back of the church to the mother who was cradling the crying baby in her arms. Everyone went silent. "Jesus won't be needing this for another year," said Becky, "but I think your baby needs it now."

The mother smiled gratefully at Becky and gently wrapped her baby in the shawl. She cuddled it close to her as Becky made her way back to her place. The baby snuffled a bit, closed its eyes and went back to sleep.

When the play was over Mrs Barnes started to collect up all the things the children had used. There were the gifts of gold, frankincense and myrrh in their luxury wrapping-paper parcels.

She piled them into the crib on top of the baby Jesus doll.

Oh, no! thought Becky. She can't do that. He hasn't even got a shawl now, and the swaddling bands aren't much use. Now all the bits and pieces are being put on top of him. It's just not fair! She marched over to Mrs Barnes, who smiled at her.

"That was a really kind thing you did during the play – everyone says it was something they won't ever forget!" She noticed Becky's worried look. "Now what's the matter?" she asked.

"I'm still worried about baby Jesus, Mrs Barnes – he's not just any old doll you know!"

Mrs Barnes looked at the crib piled high with paraphernalia from the play and made a quick decision.

"I've just had a marvellous idea," she said and carefully took the battered old doll out of the straw. "Why don't you take him home with you and look after him till next year – we'll all be sure he's in good hands," she smiled.

Becky couldn't believe her luck. Gently she took the doll from her teacher and wrapped him inside her coat, then walked home with Agatha and her mother. When they got home, Becky wrapped him up in a bit of old blanket and put him under the Christmas tree – she couldn't think of anywhere better.

When Christmas Day eventually arrived Becky had two presents from her granny. One was a small shawl beautifully knitted for the very special doll that lay beneath the Christmas tree. The other parcel was long and thin. Becky felt it and guessed straight away what it was. Agatha's first knitting needles were hers now.

Florence

Ann Ruffell

When he was old enough, Nick Hogarth wanted to be a famous journalist – one of the kind who have "by Nicholas Hogarth" at the top of an impressive column, just below a startling headline.

He had the right sort of name for it, but that was all. At the moment he couldn't even get anything printed in the school newspaper.

One of the reasons for this was that he couldn't think of anything really exciting to write. If he were a real journalist, editors would send him out on dangerous missions to report on wars or terrible accidents. Nothing like that ever happened at school. When he tried to write about the war between Anjie Deacy and Sue Bean, both girls swore they were best friends. When he tried to write about the time Paul Bacon beat up Frank Bottle on the way home from school, Paul said it was just an accident, that Frank had walked into a lamp-post, and if he wanted to argue about it Paul would punch him on the nose too.

But another reason was that he was writing things by hand. His handwriting was – well, let's be honest: at the bottom of every piece of his school work were the words, "I can't read your writing" in red biro. (Sometimes Nick couldn't read what the red writing said, but it was always the same so he didn't need to ask.)

Everyone else sent in their school newspaper articles on the word processor.

So why didn't *he* do it at school? you ask.

Good thinking, that. But there was a snag. Mr Wilkes, his teacher, said that he wasn't going to be allowed to use the school computers until he learned to write legibly.

"It's so bad that even you can't read it,"

snapped Mr Wilkes, and threw his latest work on history on to the floor.

Lots of people had computers at home, but they didn't use them as word processors. They used them to play computer games. When Nick asked his friends if he could borrow some time on their computer, they all said, "Of course – when I've finished this game." But the game never seemed to be finished. Not before the time he had to go home, anyway.

Why didn't Nick's dad buy him a word processor, then?

Because his dad was out of a job and couldn't afford a word processor. It was as simple as that.

However, it was nearly Christmas. Class Four were singing carols every moment of the day, Class Five were stringing decorations over and under and through everything you could go over and under and through, and Class Six were getting ready for the Bumper Christmas Issue of their newspaper.

"Go and get a second-hand typewriter, son," Nick's dad had said, and given him such a pitifully small amount of cash that Nick thought of saying cleverly, "Where's the money?" after his dad had put it into his hand.

So there he was, in the junk shop, looking at second-hand typewriters. There were three. One was a rather snooty grey office machine, the second a newer electric model with a burned-out motor. And there was Florence.

Florence was very elegant, in an old-fashioned way. She wasn't exactly streamlined, but her keys were rimmed with brass, and if the black background to the letters was a little sunken with wear, it only made the brass stand out like fine bones. Her carriage lever curved gracefully like a Georgian door handle, and there was a matching curve in front of the rows of type, in black, with a faded gold line running through it.

Florence sort of shone her brasswork at Nick but she was the last machine he wanted to buy.

Everyone would laugh at him if he bought an old thing like that. They wouldn't see her as an antique. They'd say she was a bit of old rubbish and probably take her apart for spares to mend their mountain bikes.

But he had to buy her in the end because she was the only one whose price matched the coins in his pocket.

He took her home wrapped up in his jumper, even though it was cold.

"Wotcher got there, Nick?" shouted Bill Bodger, one of his friends, looking over his gate just before tea-time.

"Secret," said Nick.

"Show us," said Bill.

"Don't be daft," said Nick. "You don't show people secrets. That's why they're secret."

"Got to be my Christmas present then," said Bill, and went inside to play with his latest computer game.

"Thanks, Dad. Can I use it straight away?"

There were still four days to go before the end of term: he might just have time to get an article in.

"That's a smasher," said Dad. "You did well there, son. They don't make things like that any more." He pulled his cuff over his hand and polished a bit of Florence's brasswork. "I think I might be able to find you a new ribbon," he went on. "Your Uncle Worsley left a drawer full of them; could just fit."

"Ribbon? You don't put ribbons on typewriters!" said Nick, horrified. "They don't have hair."

"Not that sort of ribbon, bird brain," said Dad. "An ink ribbon to type on."

"I didn't know Uncle Worsley knew how to type," said Nick. To tell the truth, he'd never known his Uncle Worsley, because he'd been dead half a century already. Stung to death by warrior wasps, some said.

"Know how to type? Didn't you know your Uncle Worsley was a famous journalist?"

Nick began to be interested after all.

"Is that how he got stung to death by warrior wasps?" He could just see the headlines: "Sting in journalist's words rubbed out".

"Wasps? What are you talking about?" said his dad. "Your Uncle Worsley died in hospital of a worn-out finger. He never learned to touch-type."

Nick went off into a dream. A famous journalist for an uncle! Couldn't be bad.

He practised saying, "This is my Uncle Worsley's typewriter. He was a famous journalist, you know. Got stung to death by wasps in the cause of duty." There was no reason why he shouldn't believe the person who had told him that, rather than his dad.

He shifted the small plastic Christmas tree that his dad had put on his desk to look festive, and stuck Florence on top in front of his attic room window. There was a good view from there, which was why he'd put his desk there, apart from the fact there was no other space to put it in.

The view – it was important. Important to Nick, that is.

Exactly opposite his flat, across the narrow street, was the local newspaper office, rising a little taller than the rest of the buildings. Every day young men and women rushed in and out with serious faces and ready notebooks, but what stories came out in those stiff bundles of newspapers at two o'clock every afternoon!

Nick had dreamed of starting his career of fame in those very offices across the road. Once he believed that one day the editor would rush out, waving the school paper, crying, "Who is this wonderful boy writer? I need him on my newspaper – NOW!" not realizing that the talented writer had been on his very doorstep all the time.

But even if Mr Wilkes printed anything there was no guarantee that the editor would suddenly call for Nick Hogarth. Not after Nick's dad, who used to work on the paper, had had a row with the editor and lost his job a year ago.

To Nick's astonishment, as soon as he had worked out which key was which on the type-writer he began to bash out the most amazing stories ever!

Well, to be honest, it was Florence who in-vented them. And they were wonderful stories! Nick stacked them up in a growing pile. There was the discovery of a diamond mine in Wales, which made Wales so rich that they closed their borders and issued special Welshpersons pass-ports. Then there was the story of the bomb discovered halfway up Mount Everest – known to be the work of the anti-Yeti Brigade. And there was a follow-up to that about the brave climber who defused it, having never done any bomb disposal work before.

Well, Mr Wilkes simply didn't believe them.

"Sorry, Nick," he said. "Full marks for story writing, but it's hardly journalism, is it? We need news about people we know – football matches –

who's won this year's Readathon – that sort of thing."

Nick tried, but Florence kept embroidering his stories. She reported that Jo Slavinsky, who passed his grade one saxophone exam last week, played in front of a visiting queen who gave him a castle in Spain to practise in. She reported the football team's success in the third round of the World Cup. She reported that Betsy Pickin read the whole of the works of Charles Dickens (all 36 volumes) in *one day* and could answer any questions you liked to ask her about them.

"Sorry," said Mr Wilkes. "I know journalists exaggerate, but do try to get *some* truth into it."

Nick felt discouraged. What was he to do if there wasn't any news worth printing?

On Nick's desk, Florence began to dry out. Her joints were already old and arthritic, but Nick never gave her so much as a drop of oil to soothe her aching mechanism. He said some very rude words when her shift lock stuck and half of one story came out entirely in capitals and another one, about a train robbery, came out with the number ££%&&"! instead of £357721. He shouted when the elegant lever came unstuck from the cylinder and he wrote three lines on top of each other. He kicked his desk when, after mending the lever rather badly with a piece of wire coat hanger, he realized he had done something to the ribbon so that it wrote entirely in red.

He left Florence on his desk and went back to his own illegible handwriting. When Mr Wilkes complained he said, "It's your fault, sir. You don't like the stories I write on my typewriter."

And then, two nights before the end of term, something happened. It was so cold in his attic that Nick couldn't sleep. He had forgotten to make a hot-water bottle before he went to bed and he felt too cold to get out and make one. He tossed and turned and tried to find the socks that he had thrown on to the floor but his shoulders nearly froze off before he found them.

Nick turned over wildly and heard the duvet clang to the floor. He was half-dreaming, so it didn't seem a strange noise for a duvet to make. He yanked at the corner which was still on him to drag it back, then there was another clang, and he opened his eyes.

The room was dark. There was no moon, or if there was, it was completely hidden behind clouds as black and heavy as a Christmas pudding.

A clanging *duvet*?

Perhaps he'd left something in the bedclothes, like a pen. Or even a plate, with the remains of last night's snack on it.

He turned over, to try and find a warmer part of the bed, and whatever it was clanged again.

Nick groaned out of bed and rootled blindly in the heap of duvet on the floor to try and find out what it was. Then he heard it yet again. From outside.

He nearly went back to bed, but he was going

to be a famous journalist, remember. Despite the cold, curiosity got the better of him.

He pushed Florence to one side of the desk, swept off the pile of paper, school books and homework and with the duvet wrapped round his shoulders he leaned his stomach against the wood so that he could look out.

Florence, cold and painful in her joints, had just managed to sleep, and had begun to dream of fame. She half woke, but realizing Nick didn't want her to do anything, went back to sleep to finish her dream.

Surely that was someone creeping round the newspaper offices? Nick could see a black shape – was it? – yes, actually going *inside* the little door cut into the big one through which they rolled the huge reels of paper every two months or so. Whoever it was had dropped the heavy padlock on to the ground. That was the clanging noise. (In fact he must have dropped it several times.) Somebody after the petty cash? Staff Christmas party money? It didn't matter what, *somebody* was after *something*.

There was no time to be lost. If he ran out now, and re-padlocked the little door behind the burglar, then rang the police, he could rush back upstairs and type out the story ready for printing in the morning. When the paper went out to the shops at two o'clock in the afternoon there would be his story, plonk in the middle of the page with his own name underneath the screaming head-line!

So that is what he did. He rushed across the road in his pyjamas and slippers (he forgot his dressing-gown) and replaced the broken padlock with his bicycle-chain padlock. Then he ran back and telephoned the police.

Everything happened exactly as he had im-agined it.

Back in his room he pulled Florence towards him excitedly and, peering at the cars below, flashing enough blue lights for a fairground, he began to write down all he could see.

But Florence, wrenched ·from her delicious dream, was sluggish and sleepy. Her spelling, normally superb, turned into something a five-year-old would be ashamed of. The shift lock stuck again, and the space bar gave him spaces as wide apart as those in a Sunday car-park. Florence struggled to understand what he was doing, and tried to guide his fingers like she always did before.

I am duddobf by my windwo lookubf oyt on anamaxing scene !* of the litter were sows first cross=Atlantoc swim wrote Nick, his eyes glued on the chase that was happening outside his window.

Then Florence panicked completely. By the time the criminal had been caught, and two of the policemen were ringing the bell at the bottom of the stairs, her keys were so tangled up they looked rather like a piece of modern sculpture.

"Bed," said Nick's dad after Nick had told them all about his clever padlock and the policemen had drunk the last of their instant coffee.

"But, Dad…"

"Even heroes have to sleep," said Dad.

Nick didn't believe him, but as soon as he got back into the mess of bedclothes he slept by accident.

So he didn't look at his – sorry, Florence's – masterpiece until the morning.

He had woken with a conceited grin on his face, and even before getting dressed had run to the sheets of paper, ready to dash across the road and give them to the printer.

When he saw what he had written he flipped.

He hurled Florence across the room, breaking a model ship he had taken all year to make, which infuriated him even more.

"You've *ruined* it, ruined it … and I could have been *famous* … stupid, *stupid* OLD machine!"

He sobbed and wept and raged round his room for ten whole minutes until his dad came in with a wet sponge and chucked it right in his face.

"Look!" spluttered Nick through the soapy, smelly sponge-water. He rattled the pages at his dad.

"Calm down!" yelled his dad. "You'll just have to do it again, won't you?"

Nick pointed at Florence's spaghetti-like keys.

"I buy you a valuable antique and that's how you treat it!" bawled his father unfairly. "Oh, get off to school and stop making all that noise."

Nick ran down the road. Perhaps Mr Wilkes would let him use the school computer, just this once. But when he got there this didn't seem likely because he was late and was told off more than usual because everyone was in a state about something else.

"Where you been?" whispered Bill Bodger.

"Catching a burglar," said Nick, and didn't even care when Bill didn't believe him. His life was ruined. He would never be a famous journalist now.

"Catching what?" said Bill, then interrupted himself to tell Nick what had happened to the school computer network.

"They were printing out the paper so we'd have it before Christmas then the dreaded virus struck!" said Bill.

Nick joined the group of Class Six standing round the printer.

"I wrote about the history trip," one boy – it was Frank Bottle – was saying. "I said, 'We went on a history trip to the Roman camp. We had two fights. We saw lots of ruins.'"

Nick's lip curled. If only they had let *him* write about the history trip! Even Mr Wilkes ought to admit that he could write better than Frank Bottle.

They all watched the screen. Instead of printing out what Frank Bottle had written, the words on the screen dropped down like sieved flour, and the next line of print came out with a wavy pattern on it like one of those bleeping machines in *Casualty*. Then it said quietly, *POW!* and the screen went blank.

"It's trashed itself, sir," said Paul Bacon.

"I could bring my computer, sir," said Anjie Deacy, and there was a chorus from everyone else offering their computers. "Except," she said, "it's not really a computer, it's a console and it works off the telly." It soon turned out that half the people Nick thought had word processors didn't have them at all, except for Paul Bacon and his dad would clobber him if he used it, he said.

"I could put in another virus to kill the problem," said Mrs Sangha from Class Five, who was their computer expert. "But it takes time and won't bring back the data."

"Can't we use ANY of them?" groaned Mr Wilkes.

"They're all on the same network," explained Mrs Sangha.

Mr Wilkes went spare and everyone went quiet.

"I've got a typewriter at home," said Nick, into the silence.

"I thought they went out with the Ark," said Sue Bean unkindly.

"Its keys are a bit tangled up but Dad could bring it for you," said Nick to Mr Wilkes.

"Worth a try," said Mr Wilkes. He telephoned Nick's dad, who sighed and said if he could find it amongst the junk in Nick's room he'd bring it along.

"Wonderful!" said Mr Wilkes with joy. "You don't know how much we need that machine!"

She was needed! When Florence heard that one of her keys came unstuck immediately and the battered brass began to glow beneath the dirt.

"*That* thing!" said Anjie Deacy with scorn.

"Good grief!" said Bill Bodger.

"Don't mock," said Mr Wilkes. "Paul Bacon, run for Mr Jones. If he can't get this machine unstuck I don't know who can."

"Nice little machine," said Mr Jones, who taught Class Four. "Won't take a jiffy to make her like new. Pass that can of oil."

He began to disentangle the keys, dropping tiny drips of oil into her tired joints. He cleaned the type with a little brush and polished bits here and there with his sleeve.

Florence began to feel better than she had for years. It was a delicious feeling, being pampered and looked after. She could feel strength coming back into her ratchets and her mind began to zip round, filling with new ideas.

"Gosh!" said Nick admiringly. "She's never looked like that!"

"Only takes a little bit of trouble," said Mr Jones. "Don't get anything of this quality nowadays. Now when I was a lad…"

But Nick didn't wait to hear about Mr Jones when he was a lad. He sat down and began to type his own story – well, Florence's story – about the history trip.

His fingers flew over the keys like butter and Florence's keys sped over the paper, typing out story after story, written in such an exciting way that even Paul Bacon stopped being rude. Mr Wilkes picked up the sheets as they fell from the machine and ran for the photocopier.

"Hey, let me have a go," cried Anjie Deacy. "The school computer won't write like that!"

Nick didn't mind. His fingers were so stiff trying to keep up with Florence that they felt like a five-hundred-year-old oak tree.

Florence politely wrote a story for her, but it wasn't anything like as good as the ones she wrote for Nick.

And the special Christmas edition was ready for every pupil to take a copy home. Nick's name appeared so often on the newspaper that even he blushed with embarrassment when the others slapped him on the back. And of course, the story of how Nicholas Hogarth caught the burglar was slap in the middle of the front page.

Mr Wilkes personally took a copy to the local newspaper across the road from Nick's flat. And the next day, which was the last day of term, when they were all watching Zip Theatre's pantomime and thinking of holidays and presents and lots of rows with their brothers and sisters, there was a special visit.

No. Not from Father Christmas. He had come yesterday, to the Infants' Christmas party. It was a visit from the editor of the newspaper.

Nick blushed again when the editor gave him a medal and said there was going to be a special Schools page on his paper for talented young writers. And for starters, they would run the burglar story on their own front page tomorrow. Afterwards everyone walloped him on the back and Frank Bottle's hands left a sticky mark on his jumper.

At the end of the day, Nick put on his coat then went back to the office to collect his type-writer. (The school secretary had borrowed

Florence since yesterday.)

The editor was in the office, with the secretary and the headmaster.

"Ah, Nick Hogarth," said the editor, fixing Nick with a sharp eye. "Any relation of Worsley Hogarth, by any chance?"

"My uncle," said Nick. "He got stung by warrior wasps."

"And his brother, John Hogarth?"

"He hasn't been stung by wasps," said Nick. "That's my dad, and he's at home."

"Tell him to come into the office tomorrow morning," said the editor.

Then they all laughed and talked to each other and Nick, after waiting politely for five minutes, picked up Florence with half a letter still in her and went home.

He told his dad what the editor had said, and to cut a long story short the editor offered Nick's dad his job back.

"I'll be able to buy you a proper computer next

year, son," said his dad.

Nick – well, I suppose it was Florence really – whacked out the last sentence of his Extra Special New Year Story all ready for next term's edition.

"Don't bother, Dad," he said. "Buy one for yourself. Florence will do for me."

The Caretaker's Christmas

Malcolm Yorke

Charlie Santer is a school caretaker.

He is a short round man who always wears a flat cap (the children whisper that he is as bald as a pickled onion underneath) and a khaki overall with screwdrivers and nails and string and pliers in the pockets. He also has a droopy moustache and a bushy grey beard that looks like one of those wire-wool scrubbers you use on pans.

Today, like every other day, he gets up groaning at six o'clock and has a cup of strong tea. He wipes his moustache with the back of his hand, mutters, "Nice drop o' char," and then he walks in the dark from his trim bungalow across to the school. He unlocks the doors and stumps down to the cellar where he spits on his hands, says, "Right, me beauty, let's fill your greedy guts," and shovels coke into the boiler. He fiddles with valves and gauges until the heat is surging round the pipes into the classrooms.

"There, that should warm the perishing little spadgers up – and their teachers," he mutters, wiping the sweat from his bald head with a hanky.

Next he unlocks the school gates to let in a lorry full of all the vegetables, milk, meat, flour, custard-powder, eggs, jam, fruit and gravy for the school meals.

"Morning, Ernie, are you sure just one lorry load is going to be enough for our little guzzlers?" asks Mr Santer as he helps unload the food. "Blow me down, there's enough here to feed a bloomin' city! How do those little gannets gobble their way through all this grub? You'd think they'd bust," Mr Santer grumbles to the van driver as they carry the boxes and crates into the kitchens.

"Dunno Charlie, but they certainly scoff a mountain of it each day. Woof it up like a herd of mad vacuum cleaners they do," says the van driver, and off he goes.

Now Charlie walks round the school unlocking the doors, checking there are toilet rolls in all the lavatories, paper towels near the wash-basins, and turning on all the lights. One light doesn't work so he gets a new bulb from his cupboard.

"There, now Mrs Chowdry can see what those rapscallions in the reading area are getting up to," he chuckles.

By this time it is eight-thirty and the children are starting to arrive. "Just look at them clarty clodhoppers wearing out me lovely grass," he growls as the children chase each other round the playing field. The children wave cheerfully to him and call, "Good morning, Mr Santer."

He chunters, "Good mornin' you young scamps," to them and then bellows, "Now gerroff me bafferty grass before I chew yer ears off!" The children smile back and carry on their games – they know Mr Santer well.

So does the Head, who parks her old car in the playground and wishes him, "Good morning, Mr Santer!"

"Good morning, Mrs Stern," says Charlie, but mumbles under his breath, "About time that rust-bucket heap of junk went for scrap. What a beat-up old banger! A disgrace it is, that car, littering up me nice tidy schoolyard."

Now all the staff are there chatting in the staff-room about last night's television programmes and getting things ready for the first lesson.

The bell goes.

"A bit of shush at last now we've got all them half-pint yippy-yappers inside," sighs Charlie and goes off for a big fry-up of bacon, eggs, mush-rooms, tomatoes, black-pudding and kidneys that his wife Mavis has cooked for him. He filters some more conker-brown tea through his moustache. Afterwards he burps loudly, reads the paper, does the crossword, and takes his dogs Growler and Smiler for a walk. Then he goes to scold his cacti in the greenhouse, especially the naughty ones which aren't growing fast enough.

In the distance he can hear recorders playing, songs being sung, tables chanted and children laughing. "At least we know the rowdy little scallywags are locked up for a bit," he tells his wife when she brings him coffee and a big slice of chocolate cake.

"Oh, you are an old grumpy-guts, Charlie," Mavis tells him, and laughs.

Then the lunch bell rings.

"Oh, no, surely not time to put the piglets' troughs out already!" he groans. Charlie helps the dinner ladies lay out the trestle tables and benches in the hall, and then goes for his own meat and three veg, roly-poly pudding and more stewed tea.

Suddenly all the children rush out, zooming round the yard yelling and laughing at the tops of their voices. "What a blithering horrible racket those squawky little blaskets make," Charlie complains, as he does every lunchtime. His wife chuckles, "You know you love the sound of children enjoying themselves, so don't pretend to be such a sour old lemon with ME, Charlie Santer!"

"Well, maybe I do – but just don't dare tell anybody else," he says, smiling under his wet moustache.

At the end of an hour all the children are back in their classrooms. Charlie takes a wide broom and a bucket into the hall where the floor is now speckled in crumbs, blobs of custard and flecks of potato.

"Scruffy little blatherskites! Bet they daren't do this on their mums' carpets," he harrumphs as he pushes the broom backwards and forwards and shovels up the grunge into a plastic bag.

Next Charlie sweeps up piles of autumn leaves, grousing that, "The blithering trees are almost as untidy as the dangfangled kids!" Then he goes for a snooze but is woken, as usual, by the children charging and whooping out at the end of afternoon school. "Screechifying little banshees – why can't they just talk and walk like proper human beings!" he complains.

After the school is empty Charlie helps Mrs Murphy the cleaning lady to sweep up scraps of paper, broken crayons, clay and other rubbish. "Those spuggyifying little scoundrels have been chewing gum again," he complains when a piece sticks in his brush bristles. Mrs Murphy shines up the corridors with a big mechanical polisher, then at six o'clock Charlie turns off all the lights and the heating, closes the windows, locks the cupboards, then the doors, and finally the school gates.

"Thank goodness, a bit of quiet at last," he sighs. "No more titchy rascals bedraggling up me beautiful clean school."

Tonight there are no meetings in the school, so

he can have a big meal and a bottle of beer and watch TV with Mrs Santer until it's time to walk round the grounds with Growler and Smiler to check everything is secure and there are no trespassers who need their ankles biting.

Soon it is the Christmas season, which is a busy time for Charlie. Snow falls and he has to shovel the paths clear and he groans to Mrs Santer, "All those mucky little urchins walk on me polished parquet in their wet wellies. I could chop their feet off!" She chuckles and gives him another mug of steaming tea.

He puts up the tree in the hall muttering, "Poppycock! I just know the blooming needles will bung up me vacuum cleaner," and climbs his ladder to arrange the paper streamers whilst mumbling under his breath, "What's the point – these silly loopy whatsits will only fall down again." (They don't though.)

He arranges the hall chairs and stage ready for

the Carol Service and while the children sing and act the Christmas story he stands at the back. There is a tear in his eye and he tries to hide a proud smile under his droopy whiskers.

"Lovely little concert that," he tells his wife later, "but don't you even think about telling people I said so."

"Go on, Charlie, you're a great soft lummock. You love everything those kids do but you won't admit it."

"Me! Ridiculous! Nasty little squittlers the lot of 'em," he humphs, and stumps off to nag his cacti.

On the last day the children give Charlie a big spiky cactus for a present and then go bounding off for their Christmas holidays. The teachers go out for an end-of-term dinner but Charlie refuses their invitation to join them because, he tells his wife, "All flippin' teachers ever talk about is flippin' kids!"

At last he can relax and put his slippered feet up for a couple of peaceful weeks. Bliss. Perfect.

Uninterrupted. Tranquillity.

But—

The next morning a letter arrives for Charlie with a foreign postmark.

Dear Charlie,

Have bin took bad with me back. Carnt drive nor lift nothink much so can you see your way to giving us a hand with the delivries?

Love to you and Mavis,

Dad

"Oh, dear, you'll have to go and help him, Charlie. It's important things get delivered on time," says Mrs Santer.

"Just when I could have a bit of blessed peace! Still, I suppose you're right. It IS important."

"I can look after the school and Smiler and Growler."

"And me cacti?"

"And the cacti."

"Right then, I'll pack me woolly pants and vest and be on me way."

That same afternoon Charlie gets on an aeroplane and flies hundreds of miles to the north. Then he catches a smaller plane, then a train, then a bus, and finally gets off in the middle of a pine forest covered in the deepest snow you can imagine. There to greet him is his identical twin brother Albert. He too is grumpy and growly and has pink cheeks and pan-scrubber whiskers.

"Well, it's really gradely to see you again Charlieboy, and good of you to come and give us a hand like this. Dad's still in bed with his bad back but he'll be right chuffed you're here."

They drive off through the forest in a big sledge pulled by reindeer and eventually come to a little wooden house with huge sheds behind it. Many people in thick overcoats and woolly hats are bustling about carrying parcels or sacks. Several call out, "Hello, Charlie, grand to see you again! How's Mavis? And the cacti?"

The brothers go into the house and up the stairs. "Welcome home, Charlieboy!" booms his father from the big bed. He has the same bald head as Charlie and Albert but his beard and moustache are as white as cotton wool. Folded on a chair by the bed are his red trousers, red coat, red hat and his big black boots.

"Can't get around like I used to, Charlie," he growls. "Not as spry as I was, you see, and me back's getting a bit wembly-wombly. Still, can't let the little blighters down, can we?"

"Don't fret yourself, Dad, we'll cope," say Charlie and Albert together.

"Course you will, lads. Now what about some grub and a pint of home-brew?"

Next day Charlie and Albert divide the parcels up and put them into sacks. On Christmas Eve both put on their warm red overcoats, hats and long boots; load two huge sledges; feed and harness the reindeer; then pack their maps and flashlights and thermos flasks of strong tea. Finally they go in to share a mince pie and a glass of sherry with their dad before setting off. They disappear into the dusk in opposite directions loaded down with parcels.

When he returns early next morning Charlie just moans, "I'm absolutely whackered," and falls into bed, where he snores like a hippo all through Christmas Day and misses his dinner.

"Never mind, it was a job worth doing and you did it smashing, Charlieboy," says his dad, patting him on the back.

"Well, we couldn't let the little varmints down now, could we?" says Charlie, yawning like a bull-dozer's bucket.

Next day Charlie flies home to Mrs Santer, but he is so tired after his hard work and long, long journey that he goes to bed and snores for another two days and misses New Year and a lot more fun.

Then school starts again and the teachers, the children and Mrs Murphy all come back telling exciting stories about the presents Father Christmas brought them on Christmas Eve, and about Christmas Day food, and Boxing Day and New Year parties.

"I expect you just stayed at home and put your feet up, Mr Santer," says Mrs Stern the Head.

The teachers say, "Lucky you, Mr Santer, having a nice quiet rest and never having to think about children for all that time. We do think you're lucky."

And the children shout gleefully, "Happy New Year, Mr Santer. Isn't it great to be back in school again!"

Charlie just growls, "Humph! Flippin' kids." But under his fierce moustache he is smiling.

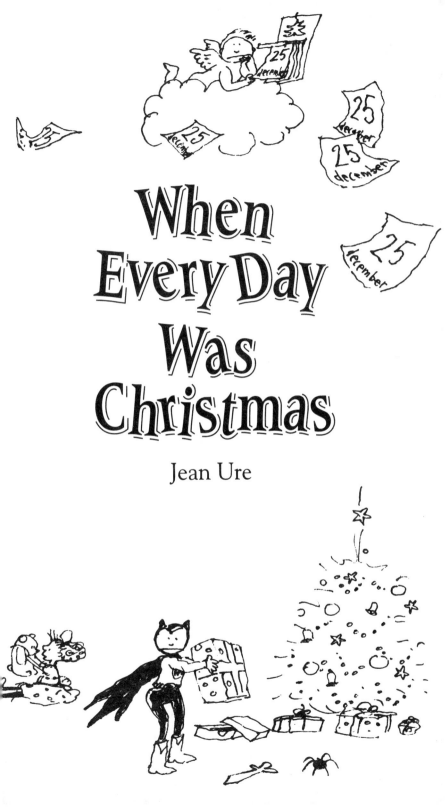

When Every Day Was Christmas

Jean Ure

~~5 days~~

~~4 days~~

~~3 days~~

~~2 days~~

~~1 day~~

CHRISTMAS!

Toby shot up the bed and switched on his bedside light. It was only six o'clock, but it was CHRIST-MAS!

At the foot of the bed he could see a large parcel wrapped in bright red glittery paper. His big present from Mum and Dad! All the other, littler, presents were under the tree, but he could open this one right away.

Toby dragged the parcel on to the bed and tore

at the wrapping paper. What was in there? What could it be?

Oh! He fell back on to his heels, his cheeks puffed out with excitement. A suit of armour! A full suit of armour, all silvery and shining! It had a real proper helmet with a visor that moved up and down, and there was a big two-handed sword to go with it.

In no time at all, Toby was inside his suit of armour and swashbuckling round his bedroom wielding his two-handed sword.

"Take that, you dog! Have at you, varlet!"

Very soon all the rest of the family were awake, including his little sister Mara, who was only four, and his gran and grandad, who were a good bit older. Gran and Grandad would rather have liked to go on sleeping, but how could you sleep with a knight in shining armour fighting battles all over the place?

"Hooray!" shouted Toby, clattering down the stairs with his sword at the ready. "It's Christmas!

Merry Christmas, everybody!"

After breakfast they trooped into the sitting-room to open their presents from under the tree. The tree was all a-sparkle with shimmering ropes of tinsel and brightly-coloured ornaments. Fairy lights twinkled and the presents were piled high.

Toby had already fingered and felt and prodded and poked at all the parcels that had his name on. There was one wrapped in holly paper, from Gran and Grandad, which was *soft*; and one wrapped in teddy-bear paper, from Uncle Ben and Auntie Lisa, which was *hard*.

There was a big oblong one from Mum and Dad, and a small square one from Mara, and lots and lots of others in different shapes and sizes. Some felt squashy, some felt solid; some were heavy, some weighed almost nothing. And Toby couldn't guess what a single one of them might be!

When everybody had their presents all laid out on the floor in front of them, Dad said, "Go!" and Toby dived in. He snatched eagerly at the big squidgy parcel from Gran and Grandad. A Batman outfit! Brilliant!

He clawed at the one in teddy-bear paper, from Uncle Ben and Auntie Lisa. A Star Trek battle cruiser! Even more brilliant!

What could Mum and Dad's one be? A game of some sort? Yes! Blow football! They could play that, later on.

What about Mara's funny little parcel? A camera? No! A water pistol! Water pistol made to look like a camera. He would have some fun with that!

By the time he had opened all his presents Toby had:

- a Batman outfit
- a Star Trek battle cruiser
- a game of blow football
- a crossword game
- a water pistol in the shape of a camera
- a spy outfit, including false beard and moustache, some sticking-out teeth and a

pair of spectacles that made your eyes look
like glass marbles
- a magic set
- a plastic spider with hairy legs
- a Yo-Yo
- a set of Space Aliens and
- a Goof ball, which made rude noises when
  you squeezed it

"Oh, my!" said Gran. "What a lucky boy you
are!"

"Shall I take your photograph?" said Toby.

"Why not?" said Gran.

He only squirted her just a tiny little bit. She
seemed to find it quite amusing.

Toby spent the morning taking photographs,
racing about in his Batman outfit, squeezing his
Goof ball when people weren't expecting it, and
trying to frighten Mara with his plastic spider.

"Go 'way!" said Mara. She was busy playing
with her own presents and wasn't frightened of
spiders anyhow, but Gran squealed quite loudly

when he dropped it into her lap, so that was all right.

At lunch they pulled crackers and wore paper hats. Toby went round collecting up all the jokes and read them out.

"What do you call a camel with three humps? – Humphrey! Why did they give the postman the sack? – To put the letters in! What are Dracula's favourite dogs? – Bloodhounds!"

Mara kept saying she didn't understand but Grandad groaned and rolled his eyes in a very satisfactory manner and Dad said, "No more! No more! I can't bear it!"

After lunch they played blow football and the crossword game, and then the grown-ups wanted to have cups of tea, which was what grown-ups always did, so Toby trundled off with his battle cruiser, zapping it up and down the hall and round the kitchen and nearly breaking Mum's neck as she came out carrying a tray.

"Really, Toby!" she said. "Don't you think it

would be a good idea if you went and sat down for a bit?"

Sat *down?* At *Christmas?*

"I haven't got time for that!" said Toby.

Already it was seven o'clock. Before he knew it they would be wanting to pack him off to bed and his wonderful day would be over. His wonderful day that he had waited so long for! He wasn't going to waste any of it by *sitting down.*

"Well, do something quiet," said Mum.

Toby went back into the sitting-room. At the foot of the tree there was a present that nobody had opened. How odd! He was sure it hadn't been there before.

He said, "Hey, look!" but the grown-ups were all drinking their tea and talking grown-up talk and didn't take any notice of him. Toby picked up the present and examined it. It was small and square and didn't seem to be addressed to anyone.

"Mum?" said Toby.

"Just a moment, Toby! I'm talking to Gran," said Mum.

Mum was talking to Gran, Dad was talking to Grandad, Mara was lying on the floor cuddling a furry animal. Well, all right, if they weren't interested!

Toby crept into a corner and opened the parcel. Inside was a box, and inside the box was a beautiful shiny stone in the shape of an egg. The stone was deep pink with creamy white swirls. Toby held it in his hand for a few seconds then slipped it into his pocket. If no one else wanted it, it would be his. His stone!

Soon after that, Mara was sent to bed. Toby glanced fearfully at the clock.

"I'll do you a magic show!" he said. "Look! With my new magic set!"

He did every trick he could find in his box of magic tricks. He waved his magic wand, he pulled scarves out of a hat (not very successfully), he made an Ace of Diamonds turn into a King of

Hearts (or tried to), and all the time the clock was ticking and Mum kept glancing at it and he just knew that any minute now –

"Toby!" said Mum.

Desperately, Toby snatched up his spy outfit.

"I can be a spy! Look! With a beard and a moustache and—"

"Time for bed," said Mum.

"Mum! *No!* Not yet! It's too early!"

Something like terror filled Toby's heart. If they put him to bed it would be the end of Christmas!

"There's still tomorrow," said Gran; but tomorrow wasn't the same! Tomorrow was *after* Christmas.

Dad rumpled his hair. "Off you go, fella! Say good night to Gran and Grandad."

Mum took him up to bed and tucked him in.

"What's this?" she said, as something fell out of the pocket of his jeans.

"That's my stone." Toby held out his hand. "It's mine!"

When Mum had gone he lay in the dark, clutching his stone under the bedclothes. Oh, why couldn't Christmas go on for ever?

I wish it would! thought Toby.

~~5 days~~

~~4 days~~

~~3 days~~

~~2 days~~

~~1 day~~

CHRISTMAS!

Toby shot up the bed and switched on the light. It was only six o'clock, but it was CHRIST-MAS!

Hang about! He rubbed his eyes. It couldn't be Christmas! It had been Christmas yesterday.

It *felt* like Christmas.

Hey! Wow! Don't say it was happening all over again?

Eagerly he scrambled to the foot of the bed. Yes, there was his big present from Mum and

Dad! His suit of armour, all silvery and shining. *It was Christmas Day for the second time!*

Toby buckled on his armour, picked up his sword and went swaggering out on to the landing.

"Merry Christmas, everybody!"

This was totally and utterly *brilliant*.

After breakfast he opened his presents from under the tree. Gran and Grandad's Batman outfit. Uncle Ben and Auntie Lisa's Star Trek battle cruiser. Mum and Dad's blow football. Mara's water pistol. Oh, but this was ace! Christmas all over again!

The strange thing was that nobody except Toby seemed to realize it. He said to Gran, testing her out, "Do you remember doing this yesterday?"

Gran said, "Goodness, I should hope not! That would mean my memory was playing very strange tricks."

Gran was old, of course. She did sometimes forget things. Mum wasn't old. He said to Mum, "I think I'm enjoying this even more now than I did the first time."

"Well, I should imagine you are," said Mum. "You weren't even a year old the first time!"

Mum didn't know! She hadn't the least idea what he was talking about.

"You make the most of it," said Grandad. He wagged a finger. "Christmas comes but once a year…"

Toby giggled. He couldn't help it. Little did they know!

He spent the morning wearing his Batman outfit and squeezing his Goof ball. At lunch he collected up all the jokes from the crackers.

"What do you call a camel with three humps? Humphrey! Why did they give the postman the sack? To put the letters in!"

They were still pretty funny.

When they had had lunch they played blow football and the crossword game. Then he took his battle cruiser up the hall and Mum came out of the kitchen carrying a tray at *exactly* the same moment as she had yesterday. Just like yesterday she sent him away to be quiet and he found the stone under the tree and slipped it into his jeans pocket. The stone felt cool and smooth. It wasn't any ordinary stone.

The magic tricks went a bit better the second time round. He was really getting the hang of things now! He pulled a couple of scarves out of his hat and the Ace of Diamonds *almost* turned into the King of Hearts. And he didn't mind quite so much when Mum told him it was time for bed. He'd had two days of Christmas and that was pretty good!

All the same, he thought, as he lay in bed holding his stone under the bedclothes, it would be great if it could go on for ever!

~~5 days~~

~~4 days~~

~~3 days~~

~~2 days~~

~~1 day~~

CHRISTMAS!

Blimey! It had happened again!

Or had it? It couldn't *still* be Christmas.

Could it?

Toby wriggled his way out of his duvet. It was six o'clock. And there was his big present waiting for him at the foot of the bed. His suit of armour. All silvery and shining. He wondered for a moment whether to bother opening it but he supposed he'd better. Mum and Dad might be hurt if he didn't.

Rather wearily he undid the parcel. Armour. Yeah. Great. He tossed it on to the floor and crawled back under the duvet. Six o'clock was too early to be up.

At breakfast Gran said, "Aren't you going to wish everyone a happy Christmas?"

"Happy Christmas," said Toby.

"My," said Grandad, "he's a little ray of sunshine!"

"He'll be all right when he gets to his presents," said Mum.

After breakfast they all trooped off to open their parcels. *Again.* It wouldn't be so bad, thought Toby, if he could have some different ones. There weren't any surprises any more. Batman outfit, battle cruiser, blow football, water pistol, crossword game, spy outfit, plastic spider –

He was too old for plastic spiders! Plastic spiders were kids' stuff. And who had given him a Yo-Yo? Girls played with Yo-Yos!

"Here," he said to Mara, "you can have these. They're rubbish."

"Well, really!" said Mum. "That seems to me the attitude of an extremely spoilt little boy."

At lunch he read out the cracker jokes.

"What do you call a camel with three humps? Humphrey."

What a stupid joke! All the jokes were stupid. And playing blow football three days running was getting to be just a tiny bit boring, and the crossword game wasn't anything special, and did Mum *have* to keep opening the kitchen door with a tray of tea in her hands just as he was going past with his battle cruiser?

Of course, she didn't realize she'd already done it on Christmas Day yesterday and on Christmas Day the day before. She didn't know that all of a sudden it was Christmas Day every day.

"Do something *quiet*," said Mum.

He went and sat down by the tree and picked up the parcel that everyone had missed. He opened it and took out his stone. His beautiful cool pink stone. He felt quite happy, just sitting there holding it.

Later on he tried a few of his magic tricks, but perhaps he wasn't in the mood because nothing seemed to go right. He couldn't even pull *one* scarf out of his hat and the Ace of Diamonds obstinately refused to be anything except the Ace of Diamonds.

He thought maybe he wasn't feeling very well.

It must be all the sweets he had eaten, and all the chocolates he had eaten, and all the dates and tarts and Christmas pudding. He had been eating dates and tarts and Christmas pudding for three days! How much longer could he go on? He would swell up like a balloon. He would go pop!

"Toby," said Mum.

"Yes, all right," said Toby.

He put away his magic set and trailed upstairs to bed. Mum came to tuck him up, as usual. Toby sighed. His fingers curled round his pink stone. You couldn't be bored with Christmas! *Could* you?

He still reckoned that having two days of it was a good idea. But maybe after that things ought to move on. Maybe it was a bit of a mistake wanting it to be Christmas for ever. Ever was a terribly long time!

I wouldn't awfully mind, thought Toby, clutching his stone, if it could be Boxing Day tomorrow...

* * *

"Toby!" called Mum. "Time to wake up!"

Slowly and cautiously, Toby opened his eyes.

"What day is it?" he said.

Mum laughed. "Boxing Day! We're going to Auntie Lisa's ... what are you doing with that stone?" She prised open his fingers and held up a smooth pink stone in the shape of an egg. "Where did that come from?"

"Dunno," said Toby. He looked at it, puzzled.

"Well, it's rather nice," said Mum. "Too nice to throw away." She slipped it into the pocket of her skirt. "Come on then, Toby, look sharp! We're in a rush as usual. I really do wish," sighed Mum, "that we could have a few more hours in the day."

Even as Toby watched, the figures on his bedside clock started bunching themselves up, shuffling and squashing until 12 had moved down to where 9 used to be and a whole new set of numbers was beginning to appear ... 13, 14, 15, 16.

Wow! It looked like Mum had got her wish. How many hours in the day were there now?

Toby thought about it. The hands of the clock had to go round twice to make a day. Twice sixteen was thirty-two. Thirty-two hours in the day! Eight more than normal!

This could be serious.

Toby scrambled out of bed and into his clothes. If he was expected to do all this extra living he'd jolly well need some extra food to go with it. They'd have to invent some more meals! Breakfast, dinner and tea wouldn't be nearly enough.

He ran out on to the landing and found Gran in a state of confusion.

"Something funny's going on," she said. "There seem to be more hours in the day."

"Eight of 'em!" said Toby. "I'm going downstairs to start eating!"

The Green Mouse

Gillian Cross

When Sally Baxter was eight, her mother and father won a prize in a competition. Christmas in Australia, for two.

"You can't go!" Sally wailed. "What about me?"

Her mother stopped dancing round the room, and looked guilty. Mr Baxter put an arm round her shoulders.

"Grandma will be delighted to have Sally," he said firmly. "Everyone wants a child in the house at Christmas."

He was on his way to the telephone before Sally could argue.

Grandma *was* delighted. "*...we'll have a wonderful time*," she wrote to Sally. "*Uncle Bill*

and Auntie May are coming too, and we'll do everything PROPERLY."

"Isn't that kind!" Mrs Baxter said.

But Sally's heart sank. Uncle Bill and Auntie
May were really Great-Uncle Bill and Great-
Auntie May, Grandma's brother and sister. They
were even older than she was. Christmas was
going to be really miserable.

When she arrived at Grandma's house, the day
before Christmas Eve, there were lists up everywhere.

- ORDER EXTRA MILK
- COLLECT TURKEY
- BUY SPROUTS
- MAKE BRANDY BUTTER
- ICE CAKE
- FIND DECORATIONS

Grandma and Uncle Bill and Auntie May were
very pleased to see Sally, but they looked tired.

"We've got lots of things to arrange," Grandma
said. "Be a good girl and read a book today."

Sally scowled. "I can read any time," she muttered under her breath. "This is Christmas."

But there didn't seem to be anything else to do. Sulkily, she curled up with *Matilda*. By the end of the day, she had finished it and read the first two chapters again.

When she came downstairs next morning, Grandma was already in the kitchen, frantically making mince pies.

"Hallo, darling." She waved a floury hand. Rather wearily. "Why don't you go and help Uncle Bill? He's putting up the Christmas tree."

Sally took a banana and wandered into the lounge. Uncle Bill was having a struggle with the tree, but he looked shocked when she suggested helping.

"You mustn't see it. Not before Christmas morning. That would spoil everything." Gently but firmly, he pushed her out and shut the door behind her.

Sally stamped upstairs. Auntie May was sitting

in the bedroom, frantically knitting something bright green.

"…purl, knit two together, knit one…"

Sally stood in the doorway. "Will you come and play Scrabble?"

Auntie May looked up and frowned. "I haven't got time to play. If I don't finish this, you won't have a stocking to hang up tonight."

"I could have a pillow case," Sally said helpfully.

Auntie May was appalled. "No you couldn't!" She shook her head and began knitting even harder with the green wool.

Sally pulled a face. She hated green. But Auntie May didn't look at her again, so she drifted back downstairs.

"Grandma – I'm bored," she said sulkily. "What can I do?"

"Oh, Sally!" Grandma had finished the mince pies now, and she was busy making stuffing, but she stopped and wiped her hands on her apron.

"Let's see what we can find."

They went up to Sally's attic bedroom. Grandma opened the little door behind the bed and knelt down, sticking her head into the cold, dark space under the roof.

"Somewhere here there ought to be –" She rummaged around. "Here we are." Panting slightly, she pulled out a big cardboard box. "We used to play with this for hours when we were children."

Sally looked doubtfully at the dusty box. It was full of battered old pieces of wood and cardboard. "What is it?"

"It's a toy theatre," Grandma said triumphantly. "Look."

She took out the pieces of wood, fumbled for a moment and then slotted them together. They made a model theatre about the size of a television.

"There are some curtains." She reached into the box again and pulled out two pieces of dirty red material. "Auntie May made them when she was six." She slid them on to the rail behind the front arch. "I rigged up those lights –" she waved at the little bulbs round the arch – "but I don't think they work any more. You'll find some characters in the box though." She patted Sally's shoulder and then hurried back downstairs to the kitchen.

Sally looked at the theatre and pulled a face. It was old. And shabby. And *green*. But there was nothing else to do, so she emptied the rest of the bits out of the box.

The big bits of cardboard were scenery, carefully drawn and painted. Sally chose a castle picture and propped it up at the back of the stage. Then she sorted out the characters.

There were three of them. They had been painted on cardboard, cut out neatly and glued on to long wooden sticks that stuck out sideways. They must have looked quite good when they were new, but there had obviously been a mouse under the roof, and all three characters were damaged.

The prince had a fine golden crown and a sword in his right hand, but one of his legs was chewed off.

The princess had a blue dress and long, curling fair hair – but only on the right-hand side. On the other side of her head, the hair was eaten away and she was bald.

And there was a witch.

At least, Sally thought it was meant to be a witch, because it had a broom and a black dress. But its hat was missing and the mouse had nibbled both its arms away.

I wish it had eaten the rest of them too, Sally thought, prodding crossly at the heap of cardboard. *They're – OUCH!*

Something had scratched her finger. She pulled it out of the pile. It was a spare wooden stick, like the ones glued on to the little figures. And it gave Sally an idea.

I'll make a mouse myself. To eat them up!

Opening her suitcase, she found her pencil box and a piece of paper. Then she sat on the edge of the bed and drew a mouse, twice as big as the characters from the theatre. It wasn't a very good mouse, because it was too long and thin, and its tail was too thick, but she didn't care. She found her brown felt pen, to colour it in.

But the brown was used up and it wouldn't do anything except make dry scratches. Angrily, Sally threw it across the room and snatched up another pen. The green one. That was certain to be full of ink, because she never used it.

Serve those silly characters right if they got eaten by a *green* mouse!

She gave the mouse black eyes and a bright red tongue too and cut it out very quickly. The scissors made rough, jagged spikes all down the long, green back, but what did that matter? As soon as it was cut out, she ran downstairs, to ask Grandma for some Sellotape.

But there was no one in the kitchen. Instead, she could hear people talking behind the sitting-room door.

"...such *hard work*," said Grandma's voice. Wearily.

"And never a smile!" (That was Auntie May, sounding quite cross.) "She's always moaning. You ought to tell her, Bill –"

Sally didn't like to walk in and interrupt. Instead, she stood in the hall and called. "Grandma!"

The sitting-room door opened a crack, and Grandma stuck her head out, looking rather pink. "What is it, my duck?"

"Have you got any Sellotape?"

"Please," Grandma added, automatically, but she didn't wait for Sally to say it. She bobbed back into the sitting-room and reappeared with the Sellotape. "There you are. Are you having fun?"

But she vanished again, without waiting for an answer.

Sally looked crossly at the closed door. "No, I'm not," she muttered.

She stomped back up to the attic and stuck her mouse on to the spare stick. Then she lay down on the floor, behind the theatre, and tried to make up a play. But she didn't know what was going to happen, except that the mouse was going to eat everyone. And that wasn't going to be easy to manage. How could a piece of paper eat three pieces of cardboard?

She pushed the mouse across the stage towards the bald princess. "I'm going to gobble you up!" she squeaked. "Yum, yum, YUM!"

The paper mouse flopped pathetically on its stick, and the princess glared back. While she was in the attic, the damp had made a dark spot on her face that gave her a stern, squinting look.

Sally waggled the mouse at the armless witch, who was propped up beside the princess. "MUNCH!"

The witch fell flat on her face.

"GOBBLE!" Sally squeaked, jabbing at the prince. He fell over too, and the princess fell on top of him.

"Stupid things!" Sally shouted. She pushed the theatre into the corner of the room and picked up *Matilda*. But she didn't manage to read much, because she was too busy thinking what a horrible Christmas she was having. Everything was wrong. By bedtime, she was feeling thoroughly miserable.

Grandma came up to hang the new green stocking at the end of her bed. "Excited?" she said.

Sally pulled a face. "It doesn't seem like Christmas at all."

Grandma patted her shoulder. "It'll be all right in the morning. But mind you go to sleep now. If you're awake when Father Christmas comes, you'll have No Presents."

No Presents was a dreadful idea. Sally snuggled down under the covers, screwing her eyes up tight. *I'll never get to sleep,* she thought. But she did. She fell asleep almost straight away, and slept very soundly.

Until she was woken up in the middle of the night.

What woke her was a voice from the corner of her bedroom. A pathetic, squeaky voice.

"Oh, dear, it's such an *awkward* dragon!"

Sally blinked and sat up, rubbing her eyes. It was very dark, and she could see her stocking hanging at the end of the bed. Still empty. *I must go back to sleep,* she thought. *Or there'll be No Presents.* But before she could lie down again, there was another voice. Just as squeaky as the other one, but very cross.

"It's your own fault. You're the one who wanted a dragon. I told you it would be a nuisance!"

"I didn't want a *miserable* dragon!" wailed the pathetic voice. "I wanted one to save us. To fly us away from The Box."

Sally couldn't see anyone, but there was a dim

yellow light in the corner of the bedroom. And no sign of Father Christmas. Quickly, she slipped out of bed and padded across the floor.

The light was coming from the theatre. The little electric bulbs round the front arch were glowing and inside, on the stage, the bald princess and the armless witch were having an argument.

"Well, this one's no good." The bald princess glided across to the floppy green shape at the back of the stage. "Oi! Dragon! Why don't you save us?"

The green shape raised its head. "Leave me alone," it said, mournfully. "I'm lamenting."

The princess sniffed. "Well, stop it. We want to escape. To go somewhere warm and sunny, before we all get shut into The Box again."

"Help us!" said the witch. "Please!"

The dragon looked sulky. "Can't."

"Why not?" said the bald princess. She stamped her foot.

The dragon raised its head. "Because I haven't

got any wings!" it said. "ALAS!" And it blew out
a great jet of flame, narrowly missing the bald
princess's one piece of hair.

"Help!" wailed the witch. "It's going to set us
all on fire!"

The princess sniffed. "You see? I told you it was
a useless dragon." She marched across to the
prince and kicked him. "Get up, you. This
dragon is a dead loss. It needs slaying."

"Give me a hand," the prince said. His voice
was muffled, because he was still lying on his
face.

The princess hauled him on to his foot and
brushed him down bossily. "Go on then. Slay it."

"No!" yelled the witch. "It's not bad. Just
miserable! Leave it alone!"

She ran at the prince, but she couldn't stop
him, because she had no arms. The prince hopped
round her, took a swipe at the dragon – and fell
flat on his back.

The princess was furious. "You missed!"

"Don't see why I have to slay it anyway," the prince muttered, staring up at the ceiling.

"Princes are *supposed* to slay dragons," snapped the princess.

"But –" Sally cleared her throat. "But it isn't a dragon."

She was trying to speak softly, but they all jumped. Then the prince and the witch both went very still and stiff, trying to pretend they were just bits of cardboard. But the bald princess marched to the front of the stage.

"And who are *you*?" she demanded.

"I'm – the person who made the dragon," Sally said, apologetically. "Only it's not a dragon."

"Oh, isn't it?" The princess stamped across to the dragon and kicked it. "Get up. Let's have a look at you."

Mournfully, the dragon uncoiled itself and stood up. It was long and thin and green, with spikes down its back. The burst of red at its mouth was meant to be a tongue, but it looked more like flames.

"Not a dragon?" the bald princess said. "What is it then?"

"It's – er –" Sally shuffled her feet. "It's a mouse."

"A *mouse?*" The princess shrieked with laughter. "How can it be?"

"It hasn't got any wings," said the prince helpfully.

That was a mistake. The dragon gave a great wail.

"ALAS!"

Another burst of flame shot across the stage.

"Oh, you poor thing!" whispered the witch. Sally could see that she wanted to hug the dragon, but all she could do was stroke it with the side of her head. She looked up accusingly at Sally. "If you made him, why didn't you do it properly?"

"That's right," said the prince from the floor. "What's the use of a dragon without wings?"

The dragon wailed again and opened its mouth. "ALA—"

"You'd be all right if only you didn't moan!" Sally said crossly.

With a hiccup, the dragon choked back its flames. "I'm not moaning," it said in an injured voice. "I'm lamenting."

"You may call it lamenting," Sally said severely. "*I* call it moaning. And it's very annoying. Why don't you smile?"

The dragon looked even more mournful. "What's the use of smiling? That won't change anything."

The witch rubbed her cheek against its head. "You could try," she whispered. "If you smile at the giant, she might make you some wings."

"She might?" The dragon's mouth widened, showing a row of enormous yellow teeth. It looked up at Sally and fluttered its eyelids. "Tra la," it said. And then it sang it, in a rusty, creaking voice. "*Tra la la la la!*"

"Well done!" the witch said proudly. She beamed up at Sally. "You *will* make him some wings, won't you? So we can all fly away."

"But –"

But I don't want you to go, Sally was thinking. She was imagining the fun she could have with them.

"Please!" said the bald princess stiffly. "You don't know what it's like in The Box. In that horrible, dark place."

The prince shuddered, and the dragon lifted its head and gazed mournfully at the cardboard box on the carpet.

Sally looked at it too. Then she looked over her shoulder, at the door behind her bed. She remembered how dark it was on the other side of the door. Dark and cold and dusty. "I –"

"Please!" said the witch.

And the dragon smiled. Hopefully.

Sally took a deep breath. "All right," she said.

The dragon gulped. "Promise?"

"Promise!" Sally said stoutly. She marched across the room and switched on the light.

When she turned round, everything was very still. Nothing moved. On the stage were three battered cardboard figures and a curl of paper, coloured with horrible green felt pen. Without any wings.

Had she dreamt it all?

What could it matter to those bits of cardboard whether she made any wings or not? It was stupid to be fiddling around with pieces of paper when she ought to be fast asleep. Father Christmas was sure to come while she was doing it.

But she remembered the dragon's creaky smile. *Tra la la…*

And she remembered that she'd promised.

Sitting down on the floor, she began to draw, listening nervously for the noise of sleigh bells or the sound of a *Ho, ho ho!* But the house was completely silent while she drew two wings and coloured them green.

Just as she was about to put away her pencil box she had another idea. Quickly, she cut out some more shapes and coloured them. A leg. A pair of arms. And a lock of long, curly hair.

She stuck everything on and waited for a moment, but there was no sound from the theatre. No movement. Oh, well...

Disappointed, she turned out the light and crawled back into bed. Snuggling under the blankets, she closed her eyes and fell asleep.

It was a tapping noise that woke her up next time.

*Clack-clacketty, clacketty-clack, clacketty-clacketty-*CLACK.

She sat up and looked across at the theatre. And there was the prince, tap-dancing across the stage. With both feet.

Behind him was the princess, with a comb in her hand. She was combing the new locks of hair on the right-hand side of her head. Sally had scribbled the curls rather fast, and she could see now that they were full of tangles. But the princess wasn't complaining. She was smiling as she combed out the knots.

Sally looked round for the witch. For a moment, she couldn't see her. Then she realized that she was down on the ground beside the dragon, hugging him with all her might.

"Wake up!" she was whispering. "Wake up, dragon!"

Slowly, mournfully, the dragon uncoiled itself and lumbered to its feet. With a huge, fiery yawn, it began to stretch its back, and its tail, and its neck and –

With a flourish and a *whoosh!* the great wings unfolded.

Sally felt the air move, right over on the other side of the room. The prince and the princess were knocked backwards, and even the witch staggered. But she was holding on to the dragon's neck, and she kept her footing.

Reaching up, she pulled on the dragon's spikes with both her new, strong arms, hauling herself up on to its neck. Then she reached down to help the prince and the princess up.

The dragon lifted its head and opened its vast red mouth. For a moment, Sally was afraid it was going to start lamenting about something else, but this time its roar was quite different.

"HURRAH!" it bellowed. "HURRAH!"

The great wings stretched and flapped. Slowly, the dragon rose into the air, with the three little figures crouched on its neck. It flew out of the theatre and round the room, rising towards the skylight. Then, with one last, gigantic flap, it was through. Out into the night sky.

Sally jumped out of bed and stood under the skylight. "Good luck!" she called softly. "Why don't you make for Australia? That's nice and warm."

She couldn't tell whether they'd heard her or not, but as the green shape spiralled up towards the stars, she caught the sound of squeaky voices singing, very faintly. *Tra la la…*

Then the dragon vanished, dissolving into the brightening sky. Slowly, Sally turned round.

The room was still dark, but the clock beside her bed said seven o'clock. And at the end of the bed was her stocking. Bulging. She ran across and turned on the light. The stocking was crammed with parcels and there was a balloon tied to the top.

A green balloon.

I hate green – Sally thought crossly.

Then she stopped. She looked across at the theatre. The stage was bare, except for four long, thin wooden sticks, with nothing attached to them. Slowly, she began to smile.

When she was sure that she was really smiling, she unhooked her stocking from the end of the bed and tiptoed to the top of the stairs.

"Grandma!" she called softly. "Do you want to see me open my presents?"

There was a mumble from Grandma's room, and the sound of footsteps. And as Grandma appeared, Uncle Bill stuck his head round the door opposite. "Can I come too?"

"And me," said Auntie May, coming down the corridor. "What a lovely green balloon you've got. My favourite colour!"

Sally smiled at her. She smiled at them all, a huge, cheerful smile that spread right across her face. "Happy Christmas!" she said. "It's going to be a wonderful day! Tra la la la la!"

And she came down the stairs so fast that it felt like flying.